THAT ONE NIGHT

A PUCKING AROUND PREQUEL NOVELLA

EMILY RATH

EMILY RATH BOOKS

WWW.EMILYRATHBOOKS.COM

*For all the thirsty bitches who love
a dirty-talking golden retriever boy.
Eat your hearts out.*

TROPES, TAGS, & CONTENT WARNINGS

TROPES

One-night stand, instalove, hockey romance

TAGS

MF, one-night stand, Seattle, cosmic connection, dirty-talking golden retriever boy, angry sad doctor girl, too much sex, it's a twin thing, no names, fuck me all better

CONTENT WARNINGS

This novella contains detailed sex scenes that include elements of choking, impact play, praise, and dirty talk.

1

RACHEL

"Have you ever been to a yacht race, beautiful?"

The Chad McBoatface hogging all the air next to me hasn't stopped talking for ten minutes. This walking Patagonia model must not be able to read, because I've got 'FUCK OFF' all but stamped across my forehead.

God, I just want to be alone to wallow in self-pity. Is that too much to ask?

I swirl what's left of the ice in my Old Fashioned, watching the cherry spin at the bottom of the glass. I'm sitting alone in this swanky hotel bar...well, I *wish* I was alone. It's all dark-paneled walls with a sophisticated nautical theme. Perfect for Chad. I snort into my glass. He doesn't notice. Am I being too hard on him?

Oh god, definitely not.

Chad's the kind of guy that talks *at* you, not *to* you. Sure, he's got the smile and the blonde curls you could run your fingers through, but he also keeps checking over his shoulder, winking at the rest of his group. They're sitting over in the corner, a great view of the Seattle skyline framed behind them. It's nearly three o'clock, and their late brunch is almost finished. They keep flashing us jeering smiles.

Wasn't he one stool over like two minutes ago? Damn it, I'm gonna have to take this pity party back to my room.

I drop my gaze to my phone and click on my inbox, tapping the top email. I must have a degradation kink, because I've reread the first three lines of this email fifty times in the last hour. It's the reason I left my own brunch early.

It's a form email, because of course. I wasted a year of my life applying to something and getting my hopes up, only to get a form email where the bot can't even spell my fucking name right.

Dear Dr. Rachum Price,

Thank you for your interest in the Barkley Fellowship, the nation's premiere partner in advanced sports medicine. We were overwhelmed by the number of truly exceptional candidates this year. The selection committee has given careful consideration to your application. Unfortunately—

I don't keep reading. I click the side of my phone and the screen turns black.

That's why I'm stuck here with Chad and not at my brother's wedding brunch. Call me selfish, but I couldn't bear to lose it in front of Harrison and his new husband and the whole extended family. So I slipped away, ordered a taxi, and came back here to wallow.

It's not like I'm missing the actual wedding. That was yesterday. The brunch today is just for those people who didn't have early flights out. I played my part all weekend long, smiling through all the events. I gave my proud sister speech at the rehearsal dinner, and danced like a loon at the reception last night.

I'm happy for him, really. He and Somchai are the definition of persevering love. But I'm sad for me too. Harrison will understand; it's a twin thing.

My flight home leaves first thing tomorrow morning. Knowing Som, he'll martial a small army of Thai aunties to bring me food for the next week to try and cheer me up. He's not even from Cincinnati, but he has connections everywhere. He and Harrison are both big-name chefs, slowly building out their empire. I can't complain when it means my fridge is always bursting with amazing free food.

Losing out on this fellowship sucks, but life moves on. For now, I need to go home. I'll let myself wallow for a day or two. My roommate will cry with me. She's basically an empath. Tess cries when actors on TV cry. She cries when cartoon animals cry. Meanwhile, I'm an emotionally unavailable, closed-off clam (her words, not mine).

So, I guess I'll give crying a try. But then I need a plan. I need to start phase two. I need—

Fucking hell.

I need Chad to scoot the fuck back right the fuck now!

He's leaning in my space, batting those blonde lashes at me. Is this his smolder? Am I meant to be swooning? How can one man fail to read every single sign a woman is giving him? I'm falling off my stool as he leans in even closer, giving my hair an exaggerated sniff.

I freeze.

"Mmm, you smell good," he murmurs. "Is that Chanel No. 9?"

Yeah, this is my absolute limit. It's time to yeet Chad back to his table. I take a deep breath, shoving Dragon

3

Rachel back inside her cage. There's no reason to make a scene. I'll just turn him down with my big girl words.

But then the fucker dares to reach out and brush his fingers down my spine. This jumpsuit is backless, so he's grazing my bare skin.

I smack my drink onto the bar, and swivel on my stool, breaking our contact. "Get your hands off me," I hiss. "It's time to go."

Chad dares to look all wide-eyed at me as he stands. "Whoa—hey, easy. What's with the attitude? We're just having a nice chat."

My nostrils flare. "Nice chat?" I say, utterly incredulous.

He huffs a laugh. "Listen—"

"Amy!" a deep voice calls. "Amy, what the hell?"

Chad glances over my shoulder, eyes narrowed towards the voice.

"I've been waiting for you for like twenty minutes. I thought we were meeting downstairs."

I spin on my stool to see a man striding towards the bar.

Holy shit, do they put something in the water here?

This guy is gorgeous too. His chocolate brown hair sweeps down over his brow as he hooks me with those hazel eyes. He's got the perfect amount of stubble covering that chiseled jaw. Not to mention the way his chest and arms fill out his too-tight t-shirt.

He's a pro athlete, I'd bet money on it. I've spent too long in the industry not to know a player when I see one. I'm guessing football. Defense. It's not just the body, it's the confidence, the look of luxury, the sucks-all-the-air-out-of-the-room effortless swagger.

Oh, and he's swaggering now, right up to Chad. He's got easily five inches on him and fifty pounds of muscle. "Is this

4

guy bothering you, Amy? Are you bothering my sister, asshole?"

I suck in a breath. *Sister?* Am I that drunk? This isn't Harrison, I—*ohhh*, we're acting. He's offering me an out. I slip into character. "It's fine. He was just—"

"I wasn't doing anything." Chad confidently squares off against his new competition.

New guy folds his arms across his broad chest. "Well, from over there it looked like you were touching my sister, and she didn't seem to like it. You want a broken hand?"

"No—"

"Cause *no one* touches my sister unless she asks for it first," he growls.

I reflexively reach out, putting a hand on his arm. "I can take care of myself," I warn. "And he was just leaving." I stare daggers at Chad. "Weren't you?"

Chad flashes me another smile. "Yeah...yeah, I gotta get going. But hey, let me give you my number—"

"Nah, she's good." My new friend glances at me. It's quick, but the look is there, the genuine concern, the unspoken question. *Are you okay?*

I give him a curt nod.

"Hey man, I can give her my number," huffs Chad. He's letting his fear of embarrassment outweigh his survival instincts. I'm not surprised, seeing as his jerky friends are sitting across the bar laughing at us. "I'm in town for the rest of the week, and there's the regatta I was telling you about—"

"Look, I don't mean to be a major cock block, but I didn't fly across the country to watch my sister flirt with some Cabela's model." He drops his gaze to me, his entire mood shifting from surly to puppy dog. "Come on, Amy," he whines, his voice softer now. "Please don't do this. Not again.

No more random bar hookups while we're on vacation. You promised we'd go see the Space Needle. And I want to watch them throw fish at the wharf."

I'm fighting my laughter now. This guy is too much. "Okay, yeah," I reply. "We can do the Space Needle. And how about I get you a dragon fruit tea from the original Starbucks?"

"Awesome." He wedges himself between me and Chad, forcing him to take another step back.

"Well, I'll just...go," Chad mutters.

But my new seat mate is totally ignoring him. He's scanning the menu QR code with his phone. "Hey, did you see they have mozzarella sticks?" he says, his tone falsely bright and cheery. "I'm ordering some. You wanna share? Oh, shit —you're allergic to dairy. Well, I'm still ordering them."

I'm smiling now. I can't help it. This guy has effectively neutralized my Chad problem without me having to be a bitch and make a scene. And now the bartender is taking his order—craft beer, mozzarella sticks, and a basket of fries with blue cheese dressing instead of ketchup.

Chad snatches his Macallan neat off the bar and returns to his table. They welcome him with hoots and jeers.

"Assholes," new guy mutters, accepting the beer the bartender slides his way.

I settle back on my stool, unable to deny the sudden shift in energy. Why do I feel nervous? This guy's presence is undeniable. It's like he's a magnet, and I'm being pulled closer against my will.

Great, now I'm the creep.

I sigh, draining the last of my Old Fashioned, and flag the bartender down. I order a hot tea instead. No more booze for Rachel.

"I'm sorry if I overstepped," he says. "I swear I wasn't

trying to be a dick, you just looked like you needed the save."

"It's fine," I reply, accepting my hot tea. I squeeze a wedge of lemon into the cup adding, "It was entertaining."

He smirks at me, those hazel eyes flashing with amusement, but they quickly fade back to sad. I want to know what this beautiful man has to be sad about. A moment ago, he was like a puppy wagging his tail, now he's a puppy sitting alone in a puddle.

"And don't worry," he adds, glancing over his shoulder towards the rowdy brunch table. "I'll sit here just to keep up appearances, but I promise I won't bug you. I know you wanna be left alone."

I pause, the cup of tea raised halfway to my lips. "What makes you think I want to be left alone?"

He snorts, taking a sip of his beer. "You mean aside from the big 'FUCK YOU' you've got tattooed on your forehead?" He gestures at my face with his hand.

I purse my lips. "Oh, so you *can* see it. Good. For a minute there, I thought it must have washed off in the shower."

"Nope. You were giving that guy all the signs to fuck right off. Not to mention you were practically falling off your stool to get away. Then I saw him touch you," he mutters, his mood shifting from sad to mad. "I saw you flinch."

I stiffen, feeling the ghost of that unwanted touch between my shoulders.

"I hate guys like that," he says, taking another sip of his beer.

"Like what?"

"Guys that think they can take whatever they want from a woman. I was serious," he adds, turning slightly to face me, those hazel eyes holding me captive. "My sister, Amy...

7

EMILY RATH

she hasn't always had the best luck with guys," he explains. "I see a woman who is clearly uncomfortable, and I sorta see red. She'd call me a protective alpha hole. Maybe you will too. But you know, whatever. Chicks always say nothing will get better until the good guys stand up and set the bad ones straight. If it keeps my Amy safe, I'll be the jerk. And maybe guys like Douche McYachtclub over there will mind their manners next time."

I gasp, setting my tea down with a rattle. "Ohmygod, shut up."

He raises a dark brow in confusion. "What? That guy was being a total douche."

I grin, brushing my hand along his arm, as I lean in with a laugh. "I've been calling him Chad McBoatface in my head this whole time."

He glances back over his shoulder and snorts with laughter too. "Yeah...yeah, that guy is a total Chad."

I settle back on my stool. We both gaze up at the TVs. There's a baseball game on next to the soccer game. The bartender brings over two steaming baskets of fried food.

The mozzarella sticks smell amazing. And I'm not *actually* lactose intolerant. If my knight in shining grey cotton offers to share, I'm not saying no. Besides, a fried stick of cheese might help soak up some of the bourbon currently sitting in my empty stomach.

"Want some of this?" he asks, sliding me a sharing plate.

I smile, reaching for a mozzarella stick. "Sure, thanks."

He picks at the food, checking his phone.

As soon as a commercial starts on both the TV screens, I clear my throat. "So...what brings you to Seattle?"

2

JAKE

It's all I can do to act natural, eating my fries and pretending to watch baseball, like I'm not sitting next to the world's most beautiful woman. I had no idea what she looked like when I walked in. She had her back turned the whole time. I saw a woman clearly desperate to be left alone, and I didn't think, I just acted, calling out my sister's name.

When she spun around on that barstool, I swear to god, she stole all the air from my lungs like some slow-mo scene in a chick flick. Her dark brown hair flowed down her back in waves, the tips golden in the sunlight shining in from the bar's wall of floor-to-ceiling windows.

She's wearing this sexy black outfit, open down to her waist in the back. The front cuts in a low "V" between her breasts. And—*fuck*—she has tattoos. They're all small, nothing larger than a playing card, but they dot up both arms, on her shoulder, a few on her fingers. I can see the hint of one on her ribs disappearing under her outfit. Cute, girlie stuff, like hearts and arrows and music notes.

And fuck me if she doesn't have a sexy little geometric

pattern low on her sternum, disappearing between her breasts. Now I'm the pig wanting to see how far down it goes. I want to lick it. And she smells so good. It's floral and smooth, but with a hint of spice.

Shit. Fuck. Lock it down, Compton.

I stifle a groan, covering it by clearing my throat and reaching for my food.

Grab fry. Lift to mouth. Chew.

Oh, and did I mention the nose ring? Yeah, she's got a fuckhot septum piercing marked by a little ring of twisted gold. Between that and her dark eyes painted black and her red lips, I think I'm in love.

And I don't even know her name.

And I'm not going to learn it, because she doesn't want to talk. She wants to be left alone. And I'll be damned if I'm gonna be that guy who saves her from one douche only to become one myself. Nope, I'm keeping my eyes on my basket of fries, my dick in my pants, and my questions to myself.

But then I feel her shift next to me, clearing her throat.

"So...what brings you to Seattle?" she says in that soft voice.

"Umm, my sister," I reply.

"Amy?"

I nod.

She smiles. "She's not about to waltz in here and blow our story, is she?"

I sigh, letting myself give in to the pity party I've been desperate to throw since I got off the phone with her thirty minutes ago. I couldn't just sit alone in my room, so I wandered up here to the bar.

Jake Compton, loser table for one.

"She's not coming," I reply. "We were supposed to meet

here as a sort of halfway point. We were gonna spend the week hanging out and doing touristy shit. But her flight got cancelled."

"That sucks," she murmurs.

"Yeah," I reply. It *really* sucks. With our crazy schedules, the time change, and the distance, I haven't seen my sister in almost a year. I miss her like crazy.

Her brow furrows. "How is Seattle a halfway point? I'm just trying to think through that geography…"

"Amy lives in Japan, and I'm out on the east coast right now," I reply. "So, it's sorta halfway. I'm closer, and have no customs, so she made me pay for the hotel."

"Whoa…that's neat. What is she doing over there?"

I glance to my right, trying to play it cool. I just need to see her again. I need to know this is real, that I'm not making her up in my head. Yep, she's still fucking gorgeous. And she's looking right at me, waiting for me to reply. She's initiating this, so I'm not the douche, right? I was totally minding my own business. She's asking the questions.

"Umm…shit, I'm terrible with the details," I say with a laugh. "Amy is the smart twin. Like, *super* smart. Two master's degrees in engineering, and an awesome job doing something with a robotics company."

She gasps, those pouty lips parting as her eyes flash with interest. "I'm a twin too."

I grin. "No way. Fraternal?"

"Yeah, my brother Harrison. He's eight minutes older," she adds, taking a sip of her lemony tea.

"Hey, I *knew* there was something about you." I grin back at her, raising my hand. "High five for fraternal twins!"

She laughs and rolls her eyes, playing along. She raises her right hand, the slim gold bracelets on her arm jingling as she gives me a high five.

We settle back on our stools, and I feel a little lighter. I want to know her name, but I'm terrified to ask. It just feels like if I do, she'll disappear like a puff of smoke.

With Amy MIA, and my new flight home not scheduled until Tuesday morning, I'm all alone here in Seattle for the next two days. Maybe things are looking up...maybe this is fate. So what if I have to put off seeing Amy until Thanksgiving? I've got a beautiful girl keeping me company, and she doesn't seem to totally hate talking to me.

"So...what are *you* doing in Seattle?" I ask.

"I'm also here on twin business," she replies. "My brother's wedding was this weekend."

"Is that why you're all dressed up?"

She nods, her smile falling. "Yeah, I had a post-wedding brunch today, but I wasn't feeling very festive. I may have slipped out. I'll text Harrison later and apologize," she murmurs, checking her phone.

She may be gorgeous, but it's also obvious that she's depressed over something. I don't want to push my luck, but I'm a social person...and I'm super nosy. I drive my teammates crazy by always shoving my way into their personal lives. What can I say? I like gossip, and I *really* like to help where I can. You can just call me Mr. Fix-It.

I really don't want to scare her away though, so I settle with a neutral, "Do you wanna talk about it?"

She shakes her head. "Just some bad news. I'll be fine. I'm making a plan."

I nod. "Plans are good. Plans are...well, I'm terrible at making plans," I admit. "But I'm really good at understanding the merits of a plan. And when plans are made *for* me, I stick to them like glue. You name it—travel plans, diet plans, workout plans. My whole life is basically one big book full of plans."

She glances at me, her dark eyes narrowing. I can tell she wants to ask. Fuck, I wish she just would. She's *dying* to ask. She's got that look. The I-know-you're-a-professional-athlete-but-tell-me-which-sport look. I've seen it a thousand times before.

Most women don't even care. It's like they've got a radar for the pros. They sniff us out and track us like we've got big glowing red beacons flashing on top of our heads. Mystery Girl is not that kind of girl. After almost ten years of this shit, I have a pretty good radar for sniffing out the puck bunnies.

"So...are you gonna ask me?" I say, flashing her a smile as I finish off my beer.

"Nope," she replies, hiding her own smile by eating some of my fries.

I lean in, giving her a nudge with my elbow. "Come on... you know you want to."

"I really don't."

"Why?"

She glances up at me, those dark eyes so open and honest. Fuck, she's stripping me bare with that look. "Because I don't want this to end yet."

Oh shit, this is taking a turn. I can feel it—we *both* feel it. This isn't puck bunny energy. In all those exchanges, I'm the one taking the lead. I pick the bunny; the bunny never picks me. This is totally different. This *girl* is different. It feels crazy to say it when I don't even know her, but she's way out of my league.

"And...what is *this*?" I say, stifling my goofy ass grin.

She holds my gaze. Her beauty is shredding me. "Okay, I'm just going to say something, and I need you to not freak out or bolt."

I stiffen, smile falling, totally ready to do both. "Oookay…"

"I'm a zodiac girl."

I groan. "Oh, fuck. Okay, umm…I'm a Taurus," I say. "All I know is that apparently that's ironic."

She snorts, trying to cover the sound with her hand. Her eyes sparkle with mirth as she mutters, "Of course you are."

"So, that means I lose, right? This is over before it begins? I should just pay my bill and leave, right?"

She holds my gaze again, her dark eyes rooting me to my barstool. My dick can't help it, he doesn't know we're not taking this any further. I'm aching in my pants. Fuck, why did I have to wear my tight jeans? Too much spring training has all my jeans feeling tight these days. I need to go up a size.

Focus, asshole.

Right, focus.

But now she's just sitting there, not making a move. Have we even been flirting? I know I haven't. I'm just being…me. This is so different than my usual charm offensive. I feel like she's the one with the puck, and I'm just waiting for her to do something with it.

Maybe I read this wrong. I'm lonely, and I'm sad about Amy, and this girl is really fucking gorgeous. I'm totally reading too much into this. She doesn't want me. I sigh. "Let me get the check. I'll see you to the elevator at least, make sure Chad McYachtclub doesn't follow."

As I reach for my wallet, she puts her hand on my arm. I go still. Like, I'm frozen solid. Just build me a marble plinth and ship me to a museum.

"I believe in signs," she murmurs, her gaze lowering to focus on our shared point of connection.

Her touch is featherlight, but energy crackles between us

with the heat of dry lightning. All I can focus on is the simple pattern of four stars on her thumb. What do they represent? And why is this touch more sensual than some of the sex I've had with the bunnies?

I can barely breathe. I swear, if this turns into a tease...if she winds me up just to laugh in my face and walk away...

"You believe in signs," I repeat.

She nods. "Yeah, I do. And right now, all signs point to me taking you down to my room and fucking your brains out."

Dead.

RIP Jake Compton, the best grinder the NHL ever had. He died doing what he loved most.

"I have a flight out first thing in the morning," she goes on. "And I don't want to be alone tonight." She looks up at me through those dark lashes. "I think...maybe you don't want to be alone either."

"I don't," I choke out.

She smiles at me again. "Good. So maybe we should..."

"I'll get the check," I say, already pulling my wallet from my pocket.

She slips off her stool as I bend over the bar, waving my credit card at the bartender. I glance over my shoulder at her as soon as he walks off to cash us out.

Well, fuck me sideways.

Now that she's standing, I want to drop to my knees. Her body is a fucking ten. No, she's an eleven. A thirteen. She's got curves in allll the right places, plus a little extra. She's curvy in the hips, and I can tell she's not wearing a bra in that outfit. Her perfect tits have some weight to them. They hang just a bit, heavy inside her strappy top. Her nipples are peaked with arousal.

My dick is twitching at the thought of flicking those

straps loose and seeing her on full display. She's got so much more than a mouthful to play with. I want to see her riding my dick. I want her straddling me, and I want those perfect tits bouncing as she cries out, her wet pussy strangling me. I want to fuck them. I want to slide my dick between them, and I want to blow on that little micro tattoo down her sternum.

Take a chill pill, you sex-crazed psychopath.

I let out a shaky breath, robotically signing the check as the bartender hands it to me.

She's waiting for me as I turn, the energy like a live wire between us. Fuck, I can't remember the last time I was this turned on. Maybe never. This girl is working some kind of magic on me.

She turns, ready to lead the way out.

I hardly know what I'm doing when I say, "Wait—"

She glances over her shoulder, the excitement dying in her eyes.

Oh shit, she thinks I'm pulling out!

I step forward, brushing my fingers down her arm. "I don't even know your name."

She looks at me for a moment, then shakes her head, her smile returning as she takes me by the hand and leads me towards the elevators. "No names. No jobs. No real life. Tonight, we're just two people lost in a city not our own." She glances over her shoulder, those brown eyes molten with need. "Come find me."

I smile wide.

Mystery Girl, I intend to find you again...and again...and again.

3

RACHEL

y pulse is racing as I stand. This is crazy. Am I drunk? I do a quick sobriety test with my back turned while he pays the check. My vision is fine, I'm not wobbling, I can walk a straight line. If anything I'm on the sober side of buzzed. The tea and mozzarella sticks are working their magic.

Of all the ways to deal with my broken heart over the failed fellowship, falling in bed with this guy is definitely the least mature. But I'm lonely, and now I'm horny, and he's saying yes. Besides, I was raised in a very sex positive environment. Rachel likes sex. A lot. I feel absolutely no shame in having a one-night stand. As long as he knows what this is, I'm saying yes too.

Plus, there's just something about him. I wasn't lying before, I'm a total zodiac girl, and I believe in signs. I also believe in energy. He's a good person—kind and compassionate. He's a giver.

I can feel his eyes on me, memorizing me. My skin pebbles. Why am I nervous? I turn around to face him and he stifles a needy groan. That sound goes straight to my pussy. His gaze sweeps over me before he turns away, handling the bill.

He's tall, maybe 6'3". I'm like 5'5" in heels, so I barely come up to his shoulder. His muscles are tight under his grey t-shirt, and his jeans are doing the lord's work. You could chip a tooth on that ass. I want to trail my nails over his skin, I want to see him shiver. I want—

He slaps the billfold closed and hands it off to the bartender, slipping his credit card back inside his wallet. I watch him tuck it away in his back pocket, wishing I could be that hand.

Girl, get yourself together.

I spin away, trying to take a breath. It's been a while since I've done this. I've just been so busy with work and life. I've been on the road more in the last three months than I've been home. Maybe this timing is perfect. I don't just want this; I *need* this. One door closed for me today, it's time to open a new one.

"Wait—" he calls behind me.

My excitement sinks like a rock in my chest.

Oh god, he's changed his mind. I came on too strong.

I glance over my shoulder, and I see his face flicker with five emotions at once—anticipation, confusion, need. Then he's pressing in behind me. "I don't even know your name," he murmurs, that voice low and sweet as honey.

My breath catches. Right, names would be good.

Or maybe not...

Signs, remember? I have a feeling we're meant to be two souls who find each other, but only for this moment. Then he'll go his way, and I'll go mine. I smile and shake my head, reaching for his hand. It's so large in mine, but I like the fit. I like the way he wraps his fingers around mine, holding steady and firm.

"No names," I say. "No jobs. No real life. Tonight, we're just two people lost in a city not our own." I glance over my shoulder, heart in my throat, as he hits me with that eager smile. He's in. He wants to get lost as much as I do.

I give his hand a little squeeze. "Come find me."

He steps in closer, fully committed to whatever comes next. I feel the warmth of his smile down to my toes. "Lead the way, Mystery Girl."

I keep my fingers linked with his as I pull him along. We're passing by the empty hostess stand when the brunch group comes strolling around the backside of a row of booths. Chad's friends all snigger when they see us. Two of them wave at me. One is tipsy enough he needs his friend's arm for support.

He drops my hand, angling himself slightly in front of me, as we let the other group pass us. I can feel him tense, as if he's ready for a fight. On instinct, I raise a hand, brushing my fingers over his shoulder. He calms at my touch, letting out a breath.

He smells so good. I fight the urge to lean in. He smells woodsy and floral. It's smooth and understated. I want to curl up against his chest, breathing in the fabric of his t-shirt.

"Last chance to get that ticket to the regatta, beautiful," Chad calls over. "Why don't you ditch your brother and come play with a real man?"

"Noway thatguyzzzher brother," the drunk guy slurs. Two of the others laugh.

Casual as you like, my new friend steps forward, offering out his hand to Chad. "I don't think I caught your name before."

Chad pauses, glaring at the hand. "It's Brad," he says, taking it and giving it a firm shake. "Brad Hollingsworth."

"Brad...right," he replies, totally keeping his cool.

I don't catch their next remarks because I've stepped in against his back, stifling my laugh with my hand and hiding myself against his bulk. My shoulders are shaking as I hold in a cackle. His hand wraps around me from behind, pressing me against him as he waves and says something chivalrous in parting to the tipsy yachting group.

As soon as they pass through the doors, he's turning, one hand on my hip and the other under my chin, tipping it up. He's grinning like an idiot. We both are. "His name is Brad."

I snort again. God, I have tears in my eyes. "I swear I didn't know," I say, sucking in a breath.

He's standing so close, it's practically an embrace. His gaze heats as he traces the features of my face. He reaches out a hand to stroke my jaw, and I feel that touch everywhere.

My breasts feel heavy and I'm starting to ache, that burning feeling of emptiness settling low in my core. It's been too long since I craved a man's touch like this. "Were you afraid you'd lose me to a real man?" I murmur.

"Not a chance, gorgeous," he replies. "You've got all the man you need right here."

I smile. Fuck, that's a good line. My pussy must agree because our girl is feeling ravenous. I'm ready to climb this man like a tree.

4

RACHEL

Not waiting another second, I spin on my heels and breeze through the doors of the bar into the interior lobby of the hotel. Brad and his group are already gone, one of the elevator cars racing towards the bottom floor. My heels click on the tiles while he moves soundlessly behind me. Aside from my heels, the only other sound is the soft jazz music filtering out from the bar.

I can see our reflections in the stainless steel of the elevator doors. He dwarfs me, standing head and shoulders taller. I reach out and press the down arrow, watching the white lights flash over the doors as a car races to the top floor to pick us up.

He steps in close behind me. "Can I touch you?" he murmurs, his warm breath fanning against my ear.

I fight a shiver of want as I nod.

His hands go to my shoulders, flicking gently under my hair, until we're skin against skin. His rough palms slide over my shoulders and down my arms.

The second the elevator dings and the doors slide open, I click on my heels inside the car, walking straight to the back. He follows me in, his presence overwhelming as the doors slide shut. There's a finality to it. A promise of everything that's about to come.

I spin around, gripping the cold metal handrail. He presses in, cupping my face. We both take a deep breath, our souls clicking into place like the gears of a machine. We exhale and I feel him everywhere. I *want* him everywhere.

"Can I kiss you?" he asks, already all but brushing his lips against mine.

I let out a needy sigh, letting go of the handrail to grip his soft t-shirt with both hands. "God yes—"

And then he's kissing me. His body covers mine as he claims all my air. I open to him, my hands letting go of his shirt to snake around his neck. I weave my fingers into his hair, arching up on my toes. There's just enough to grab and I rake his nape with my nails, earning a groan that has him pressing against me with his hips.

We're playful as we explore, our mouths opening until I'm flicking his tongue and teasing his bottom lip.

Ding.

His hand drops down from my face, tracing the column of my neck. I fight a whimper of need. I love a man's hands around my neck. I arch into him, daring him to squeeze, but he quickly moves lower and I lose that tantalizing pressure.

Slow down, girl. It's been two seconds. Not getting choked in an elevator is probably a good thing.

He's getting under my skin, burrowing deep. Our energy dances, coiling and joining. It's ethereal and real all at once. We keep kissing and I sense him with every part of me.

Ding.

His fingers trace my bare skin from my throat down between my breasts. This jumpsuit is skating that fine line between high fashion and Vegas bachelorette. The "V" is cut practically to my navel. It takes nothing for him to slip a hand inside the scrap of stretchy fabric. I shiver, arching into his touch as he cups my bare breast.

"I want you so much," he groans into my mouth, weighing my breast before he playfully pinches my nipple.

"*Ahh*—yes," I hiss in reply. My pussy is screaming for some attention, and I press into him with my hips, feeling his hardness. Why did I wear a jumpsuit? He can't give me what I need without undressing me, and there's no way I'm stripping naked in this elevator.

Ding.

"Fuck—" He breaks our kiss, slipping his hand out of my top, and all but shoving himself away from me as he spins around. He drags that hand through his tousled hair as he practically stumbles over to the other side of the car. "Gotta press a floor," he mutters.

Ahh, that's the dinging. We're just sitting here on the top floor of the hotel in an increasingly irritated elevator because we haven't picked a floor.

"Seventeen," I say.

He jabs the number with his thumb, turning around. The elevator immediately starts moving. He stays on the other side of the car, his eyes wide as he takes me in. His shoulders are heaving, and his lips are parted. The pro athlete is breathless. It's doing amazing things for my confidence to know how I'm affecting him. I step forward and he flings up a hand. "No—wait."

I blink, swallowing my nerves as I tentatively lick my lips. "Do you not—"

"Don't even finish that sentence," he growls. "You need to stay over there because, if you don't, I'll fuck you right here in this elevator and there's no way in hell that's happening. I'm taking my time with you."

Dragon Rachel purrs inside her cage. This man is in so much trouble.

The elevator dings again at floor seventeen and the doors slide open behind him. He holds out his hand, putting his body between the doors. I click forward on my heels. He turns sideways, letting me exit.

He follows me like an eager puppy down the colorful hallway. One hand is on my waist as I lead the way towards my room. I stop us outside the door, digging in my clutch for the keycard.

He leans down, pressing hot kisses to my neck. His hand on my hip slinks higher until he's brushing his thumb against my exposed side-boob—

Yeah...maybe this jumpsuit should be retired from public use.

He lets out a soft chuckle. "Room 1742?"

"Yep." I tap the keycard against the reader and the door beeps as the light flashes green. I give the handle a tug, pushing it open. "Something funny about that room number?"

"Not funny," he replies following me inside. "I think your thing about signs is rubbing off on me, that's all."

The door shuts behind us and he turns to lock it. I all but stumble into the room, kicking off my heels in the direction of the luggage rack.

It's a gorgeous room. Daddy never does anything cheap. All the out-of-town wedding guests got upgraded rooms, with family and the groom parties getting suites. This is a corner room, with two walls of floor-to-ceiling windows showing off an amazing view of the downtown skyline and the Elliott Bay. It's still daylight, but it's Seattle. The sunshine barely lasted thirty minutes. The sky is overcast now, grey clouds sitting low. It'll probably storm later tonight.

"Wow...this room is amazing," he mutters. "I'm glad my sister isn't seeing this. She'll think I'm a cheapskate, and I'd never hear the end of it."

I watch him look around. The bathroom is near the door. There's a stocked wet bar and a TV stretched along one wall, with a sofa and a pair of pub chairs framing it out. An electric fireplace is on beneath the TV, the fire crackling.

The only other wall space that isn't windows is taken up by a king-sized bed. There's enough floor space in the corner where the windows meet for a chaise-like thing. It's super soft and so comfortable, like laying on a cloud. I read there earlier, wrapped up all snug in my robe, before I left for brunch.

"Can I get you anything?" I say, fishing my phone out of my pocket and setting it down on the charging station by the side of the bed.

He crosses the room towards me, reaching in his pocket. He pulls out his phone too, setting it down on the other charging circle. The screen glows as the battery connects and I spy a picture of him on the lock screen with his arm wrapped around a beautiful girl. She's got the same dark brown hair and his piercing hazel eyes. Their grins are magnetic.

"That's Amy?"

"Yeah." He picks the phone up, showing me the lock screen. "This was us in Japan about a year and a half ago."

I smile. "She's gorgeous. It's weird, right?"

"What?"

"People always like to play that game where you wonder what you'd look like as a boy or a girl. We don't have to wonder. Harrison is proof I'd make a very handsome man."

25

He huffs, setting the phone back down. "Yeah...I guess."

I sense the sudden change in his mood. "What is it?"

His hand brushes my cheek. "I know your brother's name but not yours."

"And I know your sister's name," I reply.

"You gotta tell me something."

I fight the urge to go stiff. "Like what?"

"Anything," he replies, both his hands now in my hair. For such a big guy, he's so gentle. "I know what this is." He kisses my brow. "I know you want us both to walk away clean. I get it, and I'll play along. But I can't just..." He sighs, his fingers brushing featherlight at my collarbone. "I need you tell me *something*."

I let out a breath, giving him a little nod. He's right. This pull I'm feeling to him has to be satisfied somehow. We need to honor this connection. I'll tell him something that matters. I lift a hand to stroke his cheek. Then I trail my fingernail over the pulse point in his neck. I pause, flashing him a sultry smile. "Fine, here's your something: I could kill you and make it look like an accident."

He stiffens. "Fuck, is that—are you an assassin? Is this like a Black Widow situation and someone's about to bust through the window?" He glances over my shoulder towards the double wall of glass.

I laugh, inching closer. "No...but I do look better than her in a leather jumpsuit."

That gets his attention back on me. "I fucking bet you do," he murmurs, his lips teasing mine.

"Two more guesses." I let my hand wander, my fingers tracing down his chest. When I get to his waist, I tug on the bottom of his shirt, slipping my hand inside. His skin is so warm, and the muscles of his stomach are tight. I let my other hand wrap around his waist, slipping into the back pocket of his jeans.

"Fuck—" he hisses, his fingers digging into my hair, tugging my head back. "I'm trying to be a gentleman here, and you're being really distracting."

"You're not guessing," I tease. "Do you need a demonstration of my skills?"

He groans again. "You...uhh. Oh, *shit*—"

I slip my hand inside the top of his jeans, my fingers brushing over the marbled skin of his sculpted ass. I need to see this man naked. Need to worship him. Need him worshipping me.

He lowers his face to my neck, breathing me in before he latches on, his lips sucking on my pulse point. My heart flutters as my pussy clenches tight. I don't know how much longer I can delay this. I need physical foreplay. And then I need to get fucked. Hard.

"Are you a nurse?" he groans out, his hand slipping back inside my top to knead my aching breast.

I sigh, arching into his touch. "Not quite. But you're getting warmer."

His breath is hot in my ear, his hands everywhere at once. "Will you take it off?"

The fact that he's asking instead of telling—or just straight up ripping it off me—has my heart melting like a popsicle. Guys can be Neanderthals when it comes to a quick hookup. In and out. Fast and furious. They think they need to show off, own my body like they're owning the moment. I had my fill of that kind of hookup in college.

But I was right about this guy. That's not his style. He's sweet as sugar. I'm sure this lethal muscle machine has the capability for violence in the game, but out of uniform he's a big softie.

I stifle a groan, my mission for tonight clear. I want to

unravel him. I want to make him beg, make him crawl. And please, goddess, let him take off these kid gloves at some point and make me crawl too.

"Last guess," I reply. "Get this right, and you can strip me naked and fuck my pussy with that talented tongue."

He shudders as he sinks against me, grazing his teeth up my neck.

"You like that plan?" I tease, my fingers combing through his hair. My other hand is still inside the top of his pants, holding him to me. "Are you hungry for my pussy? You want a taste?"

"Fucking starving," he replies, his large hands fumbling with the zipper at the small of my back.

"Then what am I?" I whisper against his lips, biting down lightly on the bottom one.

He hisses, jerking down the zipper until he's exposed my ass to the room. "*Ungh*—doctor. Are you a doctor?"

I smile up at him. "Good boy. Now you know something about me."

He blinks at me, his lips wet with kisses. "Wait —seriously?"

I nod.

His face splits into a grin. "You're a doctor? Like a real one?"

I laugh. "I'm not a TV doctor or a doctor of furniture upholstery. I'm a real, honest to god, licensed-to-practice-medicine doctor."

His grin widens as he drags a hand through his dark hair. "That is so fucking hot." He huffs a laugh, shaking his head. "God, you're so far out of my league. What the hell are you doin' with a guy like me?"

He's trying to make a joke, but I sense the undercurrent of truth in his words. He's actually confused. I step in, brushing my thumb over his lips. "You're a lost boy, remember? You're meant to be finding me."

His forehead rests against mine as we breathe each other in. After a moment, he lifts away, gazing down at me with those gorgeous hazel eyes. "Can I please fuck you now?"

I take a step back and reach up with both hands, unhooking the clasps of my halter top. I drop it and give my hips a little shimmy. The whole jumpsuit slinks to the floor in a whisper of black fabric, leaving me naked. "I thought you'd never ask."

5

JAKE

I'm never leaving this room. Bar the door. Seal us in here, brick by brick. We'll leave a spot at the bottom so the hotel staff can bring us food and water and like, fresh towels and shit. But I want to stay in here forever.

My Mystery Girl—wait, scratch that—*Doctor* Mystery Girl is standing in front of me naked and my dick has just fainted from overexcitement. She's perfect. Smart and funny and so beautiful I wanna shout from the tallest building in Seattle that she's mine...well, at least for tonight.

I don't even realize I've moved until I've got her in my arms. My hands explore fast, feeling every inch of her I can, smoothing up her ribs, weighing both her breasts, skating over her curvy hips to squeeze her perfect ass.

Fuck, I love the weight of her, the feel of her—so smooth and soft, so fevered with need. She wants me. Hell, she *craves* me. Is she wet for me? I have to know. I grab her by the hips, hoisting her up. "Arms around me, baby girl."

She gasps, her arms snaking around my neck as her naked legs wrap around my waist. I'm still fully clothed and I'm carrying this naked goddess like a koala over to the bed.

I drop her down and she inches back. The placement of her hands press her breasts up and out towards me. It's too good of an invitation to pass up. I bend over the bed, my hands sinking into the mattress to either side of her as I cover her tit with my mouth, sucking on her rosy, pink nipple.

"Oh—*fuck,*" she cries, arching into me. She holds herself up with one hand, the other digging into my hair to hold me to her. I lick and tease, sucking on that full tit, feeling her pant beneath me.

"Tell me what you like," I say, popping off her to hold her gaze. "You like slow and sweet? You like it rough? Tell me what you need to get there, baby, and I'll be your new MVP."

She drops back to her elbows, her breasts still in my face. I can see that sexy little chest tattoo now. It starts between her breasts and trails down a little past her sternum—a girlie design of lines and dots ending in a simple lotus flower.

And yeah, I know it's a lotus. You don't grow up with Amy Compton, licensed yoga guru, and not know your way around a lotus. Fuck, I'm going for it. I've wanted to do this since the bar. I duck my head down, tracing the tattoo with my tongue, trailing up between her breasts.

She shivers beneath me, her knees squeezing my sides.

"Tell me, baby."

"I need—*more,*" she pants. "Stop being so damn polite and fuck me. Take me and use me until I'm a dripping mess. You can spank me, tease me, use any hole. And if you expect to only go one round, you better adjust your expectations because—"

I silence her with a savage kiss, my weight pressing down on her as I own her dirty fucking mouth. I swear to god, I've died and gone to heaven. Of course, my perfect girl likes to play. I bet she's got more kinks than a garden hose.

God wouldn't place a woman this gorgeous in my path only to have her be a plain vanilla bean. He wouldn't put her in a room with the same number as my fucking jersey. I've been number 42 since college. It's my lucky number. And now this girl is looking up at me, naked and begging for it, saying 'use any hole.'

Oh, baby girl, just you wait.

I push off her and stand up.

She pants, eyes wide, watching me.

I hold her gaze as I jerk my shirt off one-handed, dropping it to the floor. Her eyes go wide, appreciating my body. She fucking better. I've worked this body into peak performance mode, honing and shaping it seven days a week, fifty-two weeks a year since I was fifteen years old. This body is worth seven million dollars a year.

Eat your heart out, Mystery Girl.

She sits up as I kick off my shoes. Then I work the buckle of my belt, dropping my jeans to the floor. I wasn't wearing socks, so now I'm standing before her in nothing but my black boxer briefs, the front tented by my desperate dick. I'm not embarrassed. She's clearly gagging for it. Fuck, I wanna feel her gag on me. I want to feel the slide of her teeth along my shaft.

She reaches for me, but I shake my head. My eyes narrow as I do my best to memorize every line of her body. "Lie back and spread those legs wide. Show me your pussy."

She sighs in frustration, laying back on the bed. Her dark hair fans out behind her, stark against the white bedspread. With her eyes locked on me, she slowly drops her knees open. She's waxed bare. Her pussy lips open, and I'm graced with a perfect view of her glistening pink center.

"Touch yourself," I growl, cupping my dick over my briefs. His time will come, but it's definitely not now. "I want to watch you first. Get that pussy ready for me, baby."

She smiles. Taking two fingers, she sucks them into her mouth.

Oh, fuck—my girl doesn't mess around.

Her dark eyes taunt me as she lets out a needy whimper. Then she pops them from her mouth and trails them down her chest, over her sexy little tattoo, and dips them between her pink lips. She shivers at the contact, her wet fingers sliding through her slick.

This is torture, but it feels good too. What can I say? I'm a glutton for punishment. Pain is pleasure and all that. Whatever, we're all allowed to have kinks.

She's moaning on the bed now, eyes closed as she lets me watch her finger herself. Fuck, she's pushing those fingers allll the way in. "Please," she says on a sigh, circling her clit. "Please—"

My dick twitches at her plea. "What do you need, baby girl? Are you ready for me?"

"*Yes.*"

Good, because I can't wait another second. With a hungry groan, I drop to my knees.

6

RACHEL

I don't know that I've ever seen a more beautiful human. It's not just his physical beauty. Don't get me wrong, watching his muscles ripple as he tugs off his shirt is like seeing poetry in action. I want him on top of me, all around me. I want to feel the strength of those muscles working to bring me pleasure.

But his beauty goes so much deeper. He has a beautiful soul.

He drops to his knees at the side of the bed and snatches both my ankles. I gasp as he jerks me forward, dragging me to the edge. He flips my knees over his shoulders and looks up at me, his hazel eyes hooded with lust. His warm breath fans against my clit as he says, "Don't be shy, baby. Let me know if I'm doing something you like."

Before I can reply, his mouth is on me, that talented tongue swiping over my clit. I sigh with relief, sinking back onto the bed. I take a deep breath, letting my legs fall open as he goes down.

"That feels good," I tell him. "Don't stop—"

This man holds nothing back. I don't think he knows

how. If he's in, he's *all* in. I can only imagine the level of concentration and professionalism he brings to his game. He ravages me with his tongue, flicking and sucking, learning what makes me gasp and what makes me press against him, desperate for more.

My first orgasm coils tight in my core. God, he's good. I'm right there, and it's been all of two minutes. That warming feeling spreads out from my clit until my whole body is humming. I feel it down to my toes.

"Oh god—so good—right there—*more*—"

He presses in with two fingers, his tongue working double time against my clit, and I'm gone. I arch my back, hands fisting the sheets, muttering nonsense as I tip over the edge. My pussy clenches tight around his fingers, and he groans with longing, rubbing just right along my front vaginal wall. Meanwhile, my clit vibrates, the waves of my orgasm crashing against me.

In moments I go limp, my body shaky and warm as I come down.

He slides his fingers out of me, leaning up over me with need in his eyes, his face still buried between my legs. "Suck," he says, his wet fingers tracing my lips.

My core flutters as I curl forward, sucking his fingers into my mouth. I taste my own release, tangy and warm.

"What a good fucking girl," he croons.

I shiver. I typically like to be the one giving the praise, but coming from this sweetheart, it feels dirty and I love it. I love being his good girl. I love earning his praise. I want more.

I flip my legs off his shoulders and sit up.

"Was that good for you?" he asks, his dark brows raised in eagerness.

His earnest, puppy dog look is too much. I cup his face

with both hands and pull him forward, pressing my mouth to his. I don't care that his lips are still wet with my release. In fact, it turns me on. He tastes like me. Even if only for one night, this beautiful man is *mine*.

I break our kiss, brushing his hair off his brow. "Tell me something," I murmur. "Anything."

His smile lights him up inside as he kisses my chin, my cheek. "I play defense," he replies, leaving it there. It's enough to confirm my pro athlete suspicion, but not too much to give away his sport or his team. Our anonymity remains intact.

I mean, if I wanted to I could google all the pro sports teams and look for him, but that feels like breaking the rules. I decide to offer him another crumb. "I already knew that."

He stills, keeping his hands on my breasts as he lifts his mouth off my chest. "What—*how*?"

I smile, kissing the tip of his nose. "I read it all over your body the second I laid eyes on you." At his look of confusion I add, "My specialty is sports medicine."

His eyes go wide. "Oh, shit—do you work for a team? Which one—"

"Ah-ah." I place two fingers over his lips. "No more job talk. If it's all the same to you, I'd like to keep having sex."

He huffs, rolling his eyes, as he rocks back on his heels and stands. The new angle puts me at face level with the massive bulge in his boxer briefs. "Oh, yeah? And what does my dirty-talking Mystery Girl want next?" he asks, his fingers combing through my tousled hair.

My hands are already smoothing up his thighs, brushing the bottom hem of his briefs. He groans, his hand tightening in my hair. I drag with my nails over the fabric up to his hipbones and he lets out a shiver. "Don't play with me, baby girl. I'll happily stay in this room giving you what you need all night. I'll eat that pussy like it's my goddamn job. Say the word, and I won't get off my knees."

I can't hide my smile. See? He's a giver. Apparently, he's a talker too, and I'm here for it. My greedy pussy squeezes tight with excitement as my fingers brush over the waistband of his briefs, giving them a playful tug. "And if I want more than your mouth?"

He groans again, fisting my hair tight. He tips my head back, gazing down at me. "When these briefs come off, it's all over. You don't know the meaning of the word stamina until you've been with me. I will fuck you senseless and you'll beg me for more."

Oh, thank god.

I tug at his briefs again, ready to see him unleashed, but he stops me, both hands grabbing my wrists.

"Wait—tell me again you want this," he says, a hint of uncertainty in his voice. "Tell me you want...me." He almost winces once the words are out, his hands loosening on my wrists. I don't think he meant to say that out loud.

I sit back, looking up at him, my hands still on his hips. I feel him like he's part of me. I feel his excitement, his nerves, his need. There's no way this sweet golden retriever isn't a ladies' man. He's way too talented for this to be his first time. No, everything about him screams experience.

So why the nerves? Why this hesitation? From the moment we paid the bill, he's been putting up speed bumps, when all I wanted to do was drive us at 100mph straight to Pound Town. I study him, my mind racing. This is different for him somehow. Why is he doubting if I want him? At what point have I given him that impression?

Then it hits me.

He's never done this before.

EMILY RATH

Oh, I'm sure he's done hookups. What pro athlete hasn't taken advantage at some point in their career? Women quite literally throw themselves at these men every day of the week. But when they do, they know who the men *are*...or at least, they know their number, their position, their salaries and signing bonuses.

The more aggressive girls will even know their stats— and I'm not talking about their playing stats. Some of these crazies run entire websites dedicated to a player's hookups. They'll share info on what he likes. Does his cock have a kink in it? Does he like his girls shaved or natural? Does he go down?

It's demeaning and gross, but it's part of the life. The guys just have to get used to it and learn to be really careful. The groupies don't care about the athletes. They only care about getting what *they* want—a few days or weeks of being pampered, some free gifts, access to exclusive clubs and parties.

Is that what he thinks this is for me? Am I using him like a groupie?

No way.

I don't know his name or his sport. I don't know his salary. And I'm not asking for anything. I would *never* do that. Hell, I'm still in bimonthly therapy from being raised in a similar environment. That's what happens when your father is a world-famous rock star. Just one more reason I like my anonymity when it comes to my hookups. We still share a last name, and the press can be relentless and cruel. I've learned the hard way how to keep my head down and avoid all that spotlight-sharing bullshit.

I glance back up at the beautiful man standing so close to me. He wants me. He wants *this*. But he wants more. He

38

doesn't want to be used. And he's feeling out of control. I've been the one driving this car from the start.

Oh god, he feels like the groupie.

He didn't go up to the bar looking for a hookup. He went to get a drink and to feel sad about missing his sister. He's only here now because he couldn't avoid my pull, just like I couldn't avoid his.

I stand, running my hands up his sides, resting them on his shoulders. "Look at me."

He looks down, need and hesitation swirling in his hazel eyes.

"I want you," I whisper. "Not for your fame or your name. If anything, fame sends me running. It doesn't reel me in. And this isn't about your body or me getting a quick fuck," I add. "Maybe it started that way for like two seconds up at the bar," I admit. "I was lonely and sad about some news I got today. But now I want you here because you're kind and funny. I want you here because I feel a *connection* to you."

I step closer, my tits brushing his bare chest as I splay my hand over his heart, feeling his strong heartbeat. I reach for his hand too, placing it over my heart. I close my eyes, letting my heart beat under his palm. "Do you feel that?" I murmur.

"Yeah."

"Do you feel the synchronicity? We're beating in time. I feel locked in with you—"

"I feel it too," he says. "From the moment you turned around on that barstool, I've been kinda freaking out. I don't do this. I don't—I don't do feelings with hookups," he adds awkwardly. "I—this is crazy. I feel like I've got a lit firework in my chest." He leans in, cupping my cheek with his free hand, his thumb brushing over my parted lips. "Who the fuck are you?"

We hold each other's gaze for a long moment before I reply. "You already know me, I think...don't you?"

He nods, his gaze softening. "Yeah...yeah, I think maybe I do."

That truth settles between us. We know each other. Not in any real sense, obviously. We're two nameless strangers. But we know each other all the same. Sometimes people enter your life and it's a meeting. But sometimes, it's a meeting *again*. Déjà vu. Soul recognition. Whatever it is, we have it.

I know him. I'm safe with him. I *want* him.

I sink back down onto the edge of the bed and scoot back. He follows me, crawling over me with ease, the muscles in his arms taut as he braces himself. He sinks into the cradle of my hips, his hard length still trapped behind a layer of fabric. Hands on his shoulders, I pull him down with me.

Our lips meet in another kiss. This one is slower, deeper, but just as starved. I'd be content just to kiss him for the rest of the night. A great make-out session can be more intimate than sex. Thank god he seems to want more.

We work each other up as we explore with our hands. I'm no dainty, size two plastic groupie. I've got curves and I love them. Freckles, cellulite, scars. He seems more than happy with my body, gripping me under the thigh to spread me wider, pressing in with his hips. His hard cock grinds against my clit, the friction from his briefs rough and delicious.

I fight a shiver, heat building in my core. That empty ache is growing. I need to be filled. I want him inside me. Too curious for my own good, I slide a hand down his marble-sculpted chest, brushing my fingertips down the little trail of dark hair on his stomach that leads to the top of his briefs.

He knows what I want, and he tips up his hips, not breaking our kiss. I flip my hand, slipping it inside his briefs. My hand wraps around his impressive length and he groans, biting at my bottom lip.

"Fuck—yes, touch it," he says against my mouth. "Feel all of me. Take me in, baby."

I sigh, stroking him from root to tip with an eager hand. He's thick and long, his skin velvety smooth. He's going to feel so good inside me. I can hardly bear to wait. My pussy is more than ready for round two.

I pull on his briefs, sliding them down his hips, freeing his length. He rolls to his side, stripping the briefs off and tossing them to the floor. His thick thighs are nothing but muscle, dusted with dark hair. His calves are just the same, long and sculpted.

My gaze settles on his hard cock, and I'm reminded all over again that I am so deliciously straight. Fuck, I love cock. I'm literally salivating at the sight of him right now. I need to taste, need to learn what he likes. Before he can pin me down again, I roll onto my elbow, scooting down the bed, eager to taste him.

He stays on his back, stretched out and waiting, totally at ease with me. He's got one arm tucked behind his head and the other in my hair. I roll up to my hands and knees, letting myself appreciate him for another second before I sink my mouth around his tip.

"Fuck—good girl. Suck me," he groans, one leg sliding up until his foot is planted on the bed. The other relaxes, his hip flexors rotating to open himself up for me.

I eagerly tease him, licking and sucking, running my

tongue around his tip. My hand stays firm around his thick base.

"Don't play with me," he growls, his hand tightening in my hair. "Show me what that mouth can do. Own me, baby girl. Take me deep."

I happily comply, relaxing as I swallow him, feeling him there at the back of my throat. I suck, not caring that I'm making slurping noises.

"You feel amazing," he croons, his hand gentle in my hair.

And he tastes amazing, smells amazing. I'm drowning in him. His cologne must be a body wash because he smells that good everywhere. It lingers on his skin. His scent alone is making me hornier. It's warm and luxurious, woodsy, and so masculine.

God, this scent is my catnip.

My pussynip, comes the stupid thought. And now I'm snorting around his perfect cock, choking myself as I laugh at my own joke.

He stiffens, pulling my hair gently. "Hey—are you *laughing*?"

I pop off him, eyes watering as I shake my head, biting my lip.

But he can read me so well already. With a growl, he snatches me by the shoulders and drags me up his body, rolling us until he's back between the cradle of my legs. "You think something's funny?"

"No—" I shake my head, gasping as he grabs my thighs, spreading me wide.

His eyes are molten, the hazel all but swallowed by the black of his pupils. He rocks against me, his cock slick with my saliva as it slides over my slippery clit. God, I'm so wet for him.

We both groan. I fight a shiver, moving my leg to give me the right angle on friction as he grinds against me.

"Care to share with the team why you were laughing with your mouth on my dick?" he says, his voice dangerously low. "I think I need to fuck that mouth harder. Shove down your throat until you gag."

I shake my head, core fluttering at his words. "No—I mean, *yes*," I add with a vixen's grin. "But no. I was just...god, you just smell so fucking good," I admit on a breathy sigh.

He chuckles, dropping his nose to my neck as he breathes me in. "You do too, baby."

"No, like you *really* smell good," I say. "It clings to every inch of your skin and it's turning me on so much. I feel... ravenous. In my head I said it was like my catnip."

He hums his agreement, his tongue tracing up my neck to nip my earlobe. At the same time, his hand snakes between us and he shoves two thick fingers inside my cunt. "More like your pussynip," he murmurs with his own laugh, and I swear to all the gods, I've just fallen in love with this man.

I still beneath him, seeking out his gaze. He meets me. His lips are parted, glistening with my kisses. "Who *are* you?" I whisper.

He stills too. "Wait...for real? Is the game over? Are we sharing names and tragic backstories now?"

I shake my head, one leg wrapping around him until my heel is digging into his ass. "Please don't stop," I whisper. "I need you. Please. Need to feel you. Need you in me."

He sinks back over me. "Oh baby, I'll never stop," he soothes. "You're *mine*. All fucking mine." He rocks against me, lifting my leg to get the right angle as he presses in with the tip of his cock.

I'm so ready to feel him fill me up. I want him touching

every part of me inside and out, body and soul. Even if all we have is tonight, I know I'll never unhook this man from my essence. I know he feels it too.

But then he stills. "Shit—baby—*fuck*—" He pulls away with an almost painful whimper.

I gasp, reaching for him. "What's wrong?"

"I don't have a condom."

7

JAKE

Cue the fire and brimstone—the world is officially ending. Jake Compton doesn't have a condom. I scramble off her, my dick literally screaming in pain. I was right. Fucking. There. The tip was in! For the first time in my life, I was about to ride a girl bare. I was so caught up in the moment, in her, in this crazy weird magic between us, that I seriously almost crossed that line.

I can hear the voice of every coach and team nurse I've ever had screaming in my head. *Are you crazy, Compton? Safety first! Always safety first!*

She sits up as I drop to one knee, scrambling to tug my wallet from the back pocket of my discarded jeans. But I know what I'm gonna find. Zippo. Nada. Zilch. I check anyway.

"Do you have one?"

I groan, slapping the wallet down. "No."

She purses her lips, tucking her hair behind one ear. "You don't seem like the type to come unprepared—"

"I'm not!" I bark, my desperation making me feel manic.

No way am I losing out on the chance to be with this girl due to the slight hiccup of not having a condom. Mystery Girl will be mine if I have to run naked through this hotel and raid the lobby.

Okay, so that's probably not the *best* idea. My agent would murder me if those pictures made the press...only if coach didn't beat him to it. There's also our scary new team PR liaison. She's all of 5'0" and a hundred pounds soaking wet, but she's intimidating as fuck. I'm always intimidated by a woman in a pencil skirt.

"Well...do you have any in your room?"

I shake my head, letting out a mirthless laugh. "Sure, yeah, I packed a box of condoms to spend a week with my *sister*!"

I hear her laugh softly behind me.

"I wasn't exactly planning to get lucky while we were sharing the same room," I add.

She lets out another little laugh, covering her mouth with her hand. I glance over at her and she chokes it down. "Sorry," she murmurs, a smile in her eyes. "It's not funny."

"I don't suppose you have any?" I ask, hoping against hope that maybe she might've been planning to ride some-one's dick this weekend. Why does that thought conjure up such a vivid mental image? And why am I now feeling irra-tionally angry?

She's not riding anyone's dick but *mine*.

Ever again if I can help it.

Fuck, lock it down, Compton. You cannot fall for this girl. You don't even know her name.

"Sorry big guy," she replies. "I wasn't planning to get lucky at my brother's *gay* wedding...where the only people not gay are members of my own extended family."

I groan again, dragging my hands through my hair. "God —okay, what are the chances I walk out of here and come back to find you actually willing to let me back in the room?"

She sinks back onto the bed, her tits bouncing as her dark hair fans out around her. "You're cute," she murmurs, still smiling.

"I'm fucking desperate," I growl, snatching up my discarded briefs.

"I mean...I'm clean if you are."

Stop everything. Oh my god, my brain is gonna explode. If not my brain, my dick feels ready to burst too. Did she just say that? No.

Yes.

No fucking way. I've never been with a girl bare before. *Never.* It's not safe. You have to use a condom. No rubber, no ride. Right?

"We can't," I say automatically. "It's not safe."

She rolls onto her side, which does wonders for her tits. Propping herself up on her elbow, she smiles at me. "You don't need to worry about pregnancy. I have an IUD, and those are more effective than condoms anyway."

I blink. "Shit...really?"

"Doctor, remember?" she says, pointing at her smiling face. "I'm also a sexually active and health proactive woman in the age of the internet," she adds. "Condoms have upwards of an 18% fail rate, while with IUDs it's less than 9%."

My brain feels fuzzy. What kind of left-turn into Crazy Town have we taken that my dream girl is trying to use math to get me to fuck her?

"And I'm clean," she goes on. "No STIs. No chance of

one, really. It's been a while thanks to work and life and... Oh, god—" She sits up, slipping off the bed. "I *swear* I'm not trying to pressure you." She raises a soothing hand, brushing her fingers down my arm.

Is it that obvious I'm freaking the fuck out? I feel like I just finished a set of suicide sprints. My heart is racing. Pretty soon I'm gonna start sweating.

"We don't have to do anything," she adds gently. "Your health and comfort come first. Always. This has to be right for both of us. You can go get the condoms and—"

"I'm clean," I blurt out, reaching forward to snatch her arms. I pull her to me, needing to feel her close again. "I have to get tested all the time. Drugs, steroids, all the illegals. They do blood and urine tests on us like twice a month, sometimes more going into playoff season. I bet I have more thorough medical records than some of your patients."

"And you're clean?" she says with a raised brow.

"As a whistle," I reply, raising two fingers. "Scout's honor."

She laughs, the sound soft and musical. Lifting that hand with the little star tattoos, she brushes my hair back on my brow. She keeps doing that. She keeps touching my hair, and I fucking love it. I don't typically let the bunnies get up close and personal like this. We often don't even leave the bar or the stadium or wherever I pick them up. I don't like kissing them either. Their lips always feel sticky from that gloss chicks wear.

Not Mystery Girl. Her lips are buttery smooth. She has me all twisted up in knots. I've kissed her more tonight already than I've kissed anyone in years. I want to lean into her every touch like a dog. I want to curl up in her lap, my face buried in that sweet pussy, and I never wanna leave.

"I'll wait for you to get condoms," she murmurs, brushing kisses across my chest.

Fuck, her lips feel so good, soft and seeking.

"I'll happily wait. I promise, I'll let you back in," she adds, grinning up at me. "I'm not done with you yet, Mystery Boy."

I groan with my whole chest. This girl has been a surprise from the moment I walked into that bar. She's asking, and I'm saying yes. I'm saying *hell* yes. I swear to god, if this was Vegas, I'd be calling up room service for a box of condoms, some Gatorade, and an Elvis minister. That's how fucking nuts I feel over this girl right now.

She looks up at me with those dark eyes. Her black eye makeup is smudged a bit, making her look hazy, like a polaroid filter. She's got a dusting of soft freckles over her cheeks and nose. My gaze settles on that fuckhot septum ring. It's small, two thin bands of twisted gold. Is it crazy that I want to touch it?

Behind her, framed by the double wall of windows, a flash of lightning splits the sky. It cracks above the Seattle skyline, racing from left to right, branching and spiking.

She jumps with fright, spinning around. Her back presses in against me and I wrap my arms around her shoulders, holding her close. Our naked skin is warm, and she fits perfectly pressed in close against my ribs. My dick is nestled at the small of her back. It'll take nothing to get me hard again. I'm already halfway there, and all I'm doing is holding her.

I nuzzle my face against her hair and breathe her in. It smells different from her perfume. There's a faint note of mint. We stand naked together and watch as the heavens open and rain starts pouring down over the city. Thunder rumbles so loud, I feel it in my chest.

"I've always loved storms," she murmurs, her hands resting on my forearms. "The complexity, the power. Its nature showing herself to us. We dare to cage her in, but storms are her way of showing us the truth. She is limitless."

Fuck, the way she strings words together...I could listen to her talk all night. But right now, I want something more. I need to connect with her. I need to feel our hearts beating as one again.

I move slowly, keeping her pressed to me as I loosen my grip, my hands smoothing over her chest, my thumbs grazing her collarbones. She lets out a soft sound low in her throat that has my dick hardening at her back. My hands graze lower to cup her breasts. They're heavy and warm, her nipples peaked with arousal.

She presses her hips into me, and we watch the storm as I explore, teasing her nipples and massaging her. She arches her back, her hips locked against me, her head on my chest. She tips her head back, looking up at me with those sultry dark eyes, lips parted. The unspoken question is written all over her face. She wants more.

I gaze back, holding eye contact as I let my left hand slide down, smoothing over the curve of her hip, before I'm delving between her legs. My pointer and ring finger part her pussy lips, letting my middle finger slide along her slit, gently circling her clit.

She hums her appreciation, her eyes hooding with lust. I play, feeling how wet she is for me. I slide against her with two fingers, my other hand still holding her breast. She takes her hands and places them on mine, one between her legs, one on her perfect tit. She shadows my movements, totally along for the ride. Slowly, she changes her grip on my right hand, dragging it off her breast, up and up. I let her lead until my palm wraps around her throat, my fingers brushing her pulse point. She gives my hand a little squeeze, then shivers with need.

Oh god, I am dead for this girl. There's no way I'm stopping now. An earthquake could hit, and I'd fuck her in the rubble.

I shove two fingers inside her, loving the sound of her gasp. She's moving her hips with my hand, riding me. I let that hand at her throat squeeze, and she catches her breath, sharp and sweet. With a groan, I drop my mouth to her ear, biting the lobe. "You like that, baby girl? My hand on your throat, my fingers in your cunt...I'm gonna claim you, make you mine."

She whimpers, her body melting against me. I give her clit a little friction with my palm and her tight pussy clenches around my fingers.

I kiss her neck, nipping her ear again. "I've never fucked a girl bare before. Never in my life."

"Oh god," she pleads, squirming on my hand. She's right fucking there. I'm not taking her pussy until I feel her shatter again.

"Only you," I tell her, the words shredding my own heart, making it bleed. "There is only you."

"Fuck," she whimpers. "Don't stop. *Please*—"

Stop? I can't fucking stop. I'm about to give her *everything*. Every piece of me. I'm going to come inside a girl's cunt for the first time in my life. Fuck, I'm already right there. I've got cum leaking from my tip. I'm so ready to feel her clenching around my dick the way she's clenching my fingers. I don't know how I'll survive more than a few quick pumps.

God, I need this to last. Need her to want me. Not Jake

Compton, starting NHL defenseman. Not Jake Compton the playboy, the millionaire. I need her to want *me*. Just me.

"Oh—*oh*—"

Her moans pull me back to myself. I squeeze her neck, loving the way she's riding my hand, using her own to help me give her just the pressure she craves.

"Such a good fucking girl," I growl in her ear. "Ride my hand like you own it. As soon as you shatter, I'm taking you to that bed and filling you up with my dick."

"*Yes*," she chants, her hand dropping from mine at her neck to cup her own breast, tweaking her nipple. Her pussy is clenching my fingers so tight, she's ready to explode.

"That's it, baby," I say. I think she's getting off on the dirty talk. Fuck, so am I. "You know you're aching for more than my fingers. Shatter for me, and you can have my dick anywhere you want it."

"Ahh—*god*—" Her body goes still, her ass pressed tight against my thighs, her head slammed against my chest.

I curl my fingers along her "G" spot, pressing her clit with my palm, and whisper in her ear, "You're a dirty girl, who likes to get fucked. Now, *come*."

And fuck me, but she does. She comes all over my hand, her body shaking in my arms as she trembles and moans. It's all I can do to hold back my own release as she rides my hand, her pussy pulsing around my fingers. She trembles, her body going slack, and I know she's done.

I drop my hand from her throat first, wrapping it around her waist to keep her upright. Then I slip my fingers from her soaking wet cunt. She's all but dripping down my hand. I raise my fingers to my mouth, not even bothering to stifle my groan.

The taste of a good pussy on my tongue has the same effect as the first drop of a puck onto the ice. My heart stops in my chest, and my whole body goes into performance mode. It's time to play. Time to *win*.

With a growl, I grab her, scooping her into my arms. I march her the four steps back over to the bed. She laughs, head tipped back as she chants, "Oh, thank you. Thank you, gods."

I lay her down, spreading her legs as she crawls backwards. I'm right fucking there, chasing her. There's nowhere she can go that I won't follow. But she doesn't want the chase. That moment has passed. She wants me. She wants us.

My heart is in my throat, and I feel breathless as I take my dick with one hand, tracing her wet slit with my tip. She feels so good, I shiver. My whole body feels lit up like a Christmas tree. I'm hot, I'm cold, I'm a fucking mess.

Her hands slide up my arms to my shoulders before she's cupping my cheeks. "Hey," she murmurs. "Look at me."

I pull my gaze from where my bare dick is sliding against her clit.

I don't know what she sees when she looks at me, but her gaze softens, and she pulls me down for a kiss. "I'll make this so good for you," she says. "I'm yours. You've won me, I'm yours."

I've already won. She's mine.

Not waiting another second, I notch my dick at her entrance and press in.

Oh god, I'm gonna die.

Don't get me wrong, sex with a condom is always good. I'm the king at having sex with a condom. But sex without a condom is...there are no words. I'm falling and flying. My dick feels like it's found its home. She's so hot and wet, her pussy making room for me. I give a few thrusts, working my way in, and the slide of her wetness down my shaft has me ready to come in seconds. No way am I gonna last.

"Mmm," she hums, her hands in my hair, her legs squeezing around my waist. "You feel so good. So big."

I open my eyes, unaware I'd shut them. She's got her head thrown back, her dark hair splayed around her on the bed, and she's smiling. With the smudged dark makeup and the piercings, she looks like a fallen angel. *My* angel.

No holding back now. I thrust deep, burying myself to the hilt. She groans with pleasure, her hands drifting back to my shoulders. I do it again, loving the look of her breasts bouncing, those pointed nipples peaked and perfect. I drop my mouth to her breast, arching my back as I drive into her.

"*Yes*," she pants, her arms falling to the bed, framing her face. "God, I love the feel of you inside me. So full. You've got a gorgeous cock."

I laugh, popping off her tit. She's grinning too, blissed out from the orgasm I just gave her. I have to taste her. Need her smart mouth on mine. I bury my tongue between her open lips, needing to fill her up everywhere.

She moans into the kiss, and we tongue fuck, her arm around my neck. She snakes her other hand down, gripping tight to my ass. Her nails scrape over my ass cheek, and I groan, increasing the speed of my thrusts.

At the first clench of her pussy around my bare cock, I'm done. My entire body sparks like a stick of dynamite. Growling deep, I break our kiss, my hands grabbing her thighs. I want *more*. I want to be buried in this girl so deep when I come. I want to be part of her. I lean back, working her hips and thighs until she's all but folded in half, her legs on my shoulders, toes pointed in the air.

"Ohmygod—ohmygod—" she screams, her mouth open as she pants.

Her pussy is clenching me so tight. This girl is my new everything. She's so responsive to me, so perfectly fuckable. I wrap my arms around her thighs, holding her in place, keeping her squeezed tight, and I pound the ever-loving fuck out of her.

"Don't you dare stop," she cries. "Oh god, I'm right there —you're so deep—"

"I know, baby—I know—*god*—" I'm a trembling mess, my dick slamming her, owning her, as my hips give her everything I've got. My heart is racing. I can't hold on any longer. Damn, I wanted her to come again first. "Baby, I can't —I'm gonna—"

"Do it," she cries. "Come inside me. *Ahh*—" She squeezes me again. "*Now*—"

And I do. My back arches and I cry out as I unload inside her tight pussy. It's the most incredible feeling, and she takes all of me. She's squeezing me so hard, and I know she's coming too.

I shiver, feeling the last twitch of my dick deep inside her. Beneath me, she's panting, her chest rising and falling. We're both sweaty and shaking. I loosen my hold on her legs and they fall boneless to the bed. The change in angle makes my dick twitch again.

I pull out of her and we both groan. My body feels airless, like suddenly I'm a flat tire. I don't even bother trying to roll away, I just sink down on top of her between her thighs, my face pillowed on her stomach.

She sighs contentedly, her hands going to my hair. I shift slightly, grunting in a post-sex haze until I can get comfortable. She settles back, her peaked nipples happy to have the tent of my hands on them. She drags her fingers featherlight across my scalp and I let out a heavy breath.

Outside the windows of the hotel room, the storm rages,

rain lashing against the glass. Thunder still rumbles, but it sounds farther away now. The lights of the city glow as late afternoon begins to feel like night.

"Stay with me tonight," she murmurs. It's not a question.

"Yes."

As if there's anywhere else I'd rather be?

8

RACHEL

After Mystery Boy graciously gifts me two of the best orgasms of my life, we take turns in the bathroom getting cleaned up. While he's in there, I order down to the restaurant for room service. It's almost dinner time, and I'm starving. But there's no way I'm leaving this room. It feels like the moment I do, the magic will break.

I slip on my white hotel robe, pulling my hair up into a messy topknot. When I took my turn in the bathroom, I did the bare minimum to wipe the makeup off my face and remove my contacts. My vision isn't great, but its good enough to get by without bothering with my glasses. As long as he doesn't ask me to drive him anywhere tonight, I'll be good.

He comes out of the bathroom naked, totally at ease in his own skin. Sauntering across the suite, he snatches up his discarded briefs and tugs them on, which does the bare minimum to conceal the perfect roundness of his ass. Lord have mercy, how many squats does it take to get glutes that juicy? All the ladies need to know.

I stifle a grin, busying myself with looking for the TV remote.

He joins me on the sofa, sinking down with a soft groan. He sits right next to me, not caring that there's a whole other end. He grabs my legs, flipping me until I'm partially in his lap. His calloused thumb rubs little circles on my ankle as he visibly relaxes. He just needs to be touching me. I understand the sentiment; I'm feeling the same way about him.

"I ordered down for some room service. Hope you don't mind steak."

He smiles, his head tipped back against the back of the sofa, eyes closed. "Sounds perfect."

I flip the channel to SportsCenter. Below the TV, the electric fire burns. I took the time to turn on a few lamps too. This end of the suite is now bathed in golden light, while the far end near the windows is dark and stormy. The shadows of the rain dance across the rumpled white bedspread. I love the contrast of feeling warm and bright in his arms while a cold, grey storm rages all around us.

I feel his eyes on me and flash him a soft smile.

He's casually rubbing my foot, working his thumbs in circles over my arch. "Tell me something else." He reaches over with one hand, flicking at my robe. The "V" opens a bit more, and he brushes his finger down my chest tattoo. "Tell me about this. What does it mean?"

I huff a laugh, stretching out a bit. "It means I was fifteen and high on shrooms at a music festival and a guy named Hector had a tattoo gun."

He stills, glancing my way with a raised brow. "Fifteen, huh?"

I shrug. "I had a rather unorthodox upbringing."

I don't mention that the festival was Coachella or that my dad's band was headlining...or that the shrooms were stolen from my dad's personal stash. What can I say? I was a rebellious teen. Angry and bitter, I was practically a caricature of a rock star's spoiled rotten kid. It took a while for me to figure out the balance between privilege and purpose. I wasted way too many years thinking everything in life was going to be handed to me because of my last name.

Harrison caught on much quicker. He may have used daddy's name to secure himself a start in the culinary industry, but he's built everything he has on hard work and skill. I've spent years playing catch-up, fighting tooth and nail to prove I can earn my own way too.

That's why losing this fellowship hurts so fucking much. I wanted it. I fought for it. I powered through college in two and a half years with a degree in kinesiology. I finished med school in four, specializing in sports medicine.

Now I'm finishing up my second year of residency at one of the best hip and knee centers in the country. It's an amazing blend of physical therapy and orthopedic injury care, which is perfect for me. I love the balance of using proactive physical therapy to protect *against* injury, rather than only cleaning up the mess once injuries happen.

The Barkley Fellowship was going to be the thing to launch me fully into the highest level of sports medicine. It pairs doctors with sports teams from the NBA to the NHL. Ten months of hands-on experience working with the best orthopedic specialists and physical therapists in the world, who work on the world's top performing athletes.

The last three applicants to apply from my program all won. All three now have permanent positions on pro teams. And my mentor said I was a shoe-in. He says he's never seen a more natural talent. I don't know what I'm going to say to him. How will I tell him his record is broken, thanks to me?

Fuck, my therapist is going to have a field day with this.

My debilitating fear of disappointing authority figures rears her ugly head again.

"Hey..."

I raise my gaze off my knees. He's looking at me with such tenderness, such open curiosity.

"You wanna talk about it?"

I shrug. Maybe I'll feel better if I spill my soul. I open my mouth and there's a sharp knock at the door.

"Room service!"

He smirks. "Saved by the bellhop."

As I go to get up, he puts a hand on my knee.

"Stay. I'll get it." He wiggles out from under my legs, trotting over to the door. He disappears behind the corner, and I hear him talking to the delivery person.

A skinny guy in a hotel polo shirt comes in pushing a cart. "Evening, ma'am. Where do you want it?"

IN MINUTES, WE'VE GOT A FEAST SPREAD ACROSS THE LOW GLASS table—filet mignon, broccoli and loaded potatoes, fresh bread with butter, a sharable salad, a bottle of pinot noir with two glasses, two large bottles of electrolyte water, and two orders of blueberry bread pudding drizzled with caramel sauce. We sit on the floor between the sofa and the table, sharing it all.

For over an hour we talk about everything and nothing. Amy is his only sibling. They had an older brother who died of a rare heart condition before he and Amy were born. Apparently, his best friend has a dog and he wants to steal it. He swears the dog likes him better.

I tell him a bit about Harrison's wedding. He's curious about the way we blended in Thai customs to honor

Somchai's family. There was a beautiful making merit cere-
mony yesterday morning to start the festivities. Nine monks
from the downtown Buddhist temple came to chant prayers
and offer blessings.

"And don't get me started on the food," I say.

He hums, his mouth full of bread pudding. Once he
swallows he says, "I assume it was pretty good then?"

I grin, taking my time with my own food. I'm actually
cutting my steak. He just inhaled his. "I think the word that
comes to mind is *orgasmic*," I reply with a wink.

"Oh, don't play with me," he groans, setting his fork
down. "If you're about to say your dinner last night was
better than the three orgasms I've given you tonight, you're
gonna make me cry."

He lunges, wrapping his arm around me and pulling me
into his lap as I laugh, squirming to get away. I mean, I don't
try very hard.

"Is that what you want?" he growls, his hand diving
inside the open slit of my robe to cup my breast and tweak
my nipple. "Do you want to see a grown man cry into his
blueberry pie?"

I giggle, still squirming. "It's bread pudding—"

"I don't care what it's called. It's fucking delicious. But
you taste better," he adds, nipping at my ear. His other hand
slides up my thigh, cupping me between my legs.

I sigh. This doesn't feel so playful anymore.

"Open," he growls, his lips sucking on the sensitive skin
behind my ear.

My legs fall open for him as if I'm a genie who can only
do her master's bidding.

"Good girl," he murmurs, playing with my clit. "So wet
for me. Are you always this wet? God, I hope not," he

answers. "I want you like this for me. *Only* me. Say that you're mine."

I shiver, fighting the urge to move my hips in time with his fingers. "I'm yours."

"Fuck, I have to have you again," he groans. "Please say I can have you again. Need you." He's already pushing me off his lap as I pant out a desperate yes. "Hands and knees, baby girl," he says, jerking on the tie of my robe.

We're wedged between the sofa and the coffee table, but I'm determined to make this work. I can't wait another second to have him either. I scramble onto my hands and knees, facing the windowed wall. Behind me, he flips up my robe, exposing my ass. He bends over me, his hand curling between my legs to finger me again.

"Spread a bit, baby. You know how big I am."

I flash him another teasing grin. "Someone's feeling cocky."

He laughs, grabbing my jaw and giving me a kiss that tastes like caramel sauce. "Yeah, *you*. Right now. You're about to be so full of my cock. You'll feel me everywhere. I want you just like this. Down on your elbows," he says, putting a little pressure on my back with his hand. "Show me this sweet pussy."

I drop down to my elbows, my face resting on my folded forearms. It leaves my ass sticking up in the air, his for the taking. God, I love this angle. Some girls say doggy style is over-rated, but for me? Lord, I *live* for it. I love feeling a dick driving in so deep. With his gorgeous cock, he's going to hit me just right.

"Such a good fucking girl," he praises, notching his cock at my entrance. My pussy clenches with eagerness as he pushes in. I gasp at the fullness, fighting a whimper as he holds tight to my hips. He works himself in me slowly, letting me adjust to his length as he goes deeper.

"You feel amazing," I murmur, ready to chase this feeling of fullness, of being made whole. "You make *me* feel amazing. Please don't stop."

He stills, bending over me. His fingers brush gently along the line of my jaw. "Look at me, baby."

I glance up at him, my heart stilling in my chest. He's towering over me, owning me. We're locked together with more than just our bodies. I feel him everywhere.

"Say the word, and I'll never stop." His voice is so earnest, his tone so eager.

Tears sting my eyes as I gaze up at him. "Never stop."

And he doesn't.

AFTER OUR MARATHON FLOOR SEX, WHICH TURNED INTO SOFA sex, we collapse against each other, me pinned under him, bearing his full weight. It's like snuggling under the world's sexiest weighted blanket. My nipples are sore from the way he's been tweaking and sucking them, and his cum is sticky between my legs. I love it.

He falls asleep mumbling something about a bad call on the TV, his face nuzzled against my breasts. I must fall asleep at some point too because I wake up a few hours later to find him gone. I'm alone on the sofa, my robe draped over me like a blanket. The TV is off, but the fireplace is still on. I sit up and my robe falls around my waist, my bare breasts pebbling in the cool air.

Did he leave without a word? My heart squeezes tight. One night with this guy, and I feel ready to rethink everything. I wanted him to know my name. I wanted to give him my number. Maybe this could have been more. Maybe—

But now I'll never know.

I fight the tears stinging my eyes, but that's when I hear the toilet. After a few moments, there's the sound of running water at the sink. He's just in the bathroom. The air slips gratefully from my lungs and I glance over the back of the sofa. His jeans are still in a pile on the floor next to his shoes. So is my jumpsuit and his shirt.

I sink back against the edge of the sofa with relief. Well, my *heart* feels relief. My mind is buzzing like a hive of bees. This is beyond crazy. I'm feeling way too much for this guy. I feel weightless, like an untethered hot air balloon.

Meanwhile, my whole body feels boneless from too much amazing sex. Is there such a thing as too much sex? There's a pleasant soreness between my legs and I'm losing count of my orgasms. Five? I think there may have been a sneaky mini sixth one in there. I was mid-orgasm, and the jerk slapped my clit. Boom went the dynamite.

That was the "something" he learned about me during this last round. Now Mystery Boy knows I appreciate choking *and* slapping. If we get to bondage tonight, I suppose I should just pack it in and marry him. I'll learn his name at the altar.

I slip off the sofa, my robe dropping to the floor, and tiptoe naked over to the bed. I check the time on my phone. 3:00AM. I have to leave for the airport in four hours.

I've missed a ton of messages. My roommate Tess sent a text and called twice. Daddy texted. And mom. They were both asking what happened to me at the brunch, wondering if I'm okay. Two texts from Harrison. A "U OK?" and a GIF of Moira Rose wearing that weird head pillow thing. Good, I'd rather him think I was too hungover from the wedding last night and not too embarrassed by my fellowship failure.

I shoot off a quick round of texts. One to Tess saying I'll call her tomorrow and one to the Price Family group chat with mom, daddy, and Harrison. I smile when I see someone has already added Som.

I make sure my phone alarm is set and put it back on the charging pad. I gaze out the wall of glass. The storm is over, but everything is still wet. The whole city glistens, the lights of downtown Seattle hazy around the edges. I pad around the bed over to the window, arms crossed under my breasts.

Behind me, the door to the bathroom opens.

"Shit, did I wake you?" he calls.

I shake my head.

He joins me at the window, wrapping me in his arms. I settle against his warm skin. The juxtaposition of his warmth with the cold air from the glass wall gives me a chill. He rubs the inside of my wrist with his thumb, bending down to kiss my shoulder.

I sigh, so comfortable in his embrace.

"I love cities at night," he murmurs in my ear.

I smile. "Is that your new something?"

He chuckles. "Yeah, I guess so. It's one of my favorite parts of all the travel I get to do. I love skylines. I love the way they have a shape...like a silhouette, you know. Like, a woman's body. You can memorize it. You can see just the silhouette of Seattle and you know it."

I hum low in my throat. "Because of the Space Needle."

"Yeah." He kisses my shoulder again.

I lean forward a bit, peering through the buildings. "I think you can see Pike Place from here."

He presses in behind me, following the point of my finger against the glass. "Yeah...I think you're right. Hey—"

He brushes his hand over my hair, giving my messy topknot a little tug to tip my head back. I gaze up at him and he's smiling. "You wanna go there in the morning before your flight? You still owe me a dragon fruit tea, remember? I mean, I'm gonna make you change the order to a grande americano, but still—"

"I can't," I say quickly. "I have to be to the airport in four hours."

My words settle between us. My head spoke them faster than my heart could scream *stop*.

He's still as stone behind me, his body tense. After a minute, he lets out a heavy sigh, his body curling around me. "Stay."

I close my eyes tight, heart racing.

"Stay the week with me," he says, kissing my shoulder again, his warm breath fanning over my skin. "Change your flight. I'll pay for it. The hotel is already reserved. I'll cover everything. Just—don't leave yet."

I shake my head, my body at war with itself. "I can't stay. I've got a job and a life and...obligations."

Yeah, like the obligation to let Doctor Halla know I'm a failure and that I won't be his next sports medicine rising star. He was planning on me winning the fellowship, so he was already interviewing candidates to take over my residency position. Now I get to crawl back to Cincinnati and beg him not to give my spot away.

"Well...then stay one more day," he urges, turning me in his arms. He puts a firm hand under my chin, tipping my face up. "I don't want you to go. I don't want this to end so soon. Give me one more day."

Why does it feel like my heart is breaking? I wrap my hand gently around his wrist. "Listen, my life right now is... chaotic. I got some really shitty news today about a job, and

66

I honestly don't know what comes next. I have to go home. I have to deal with this, and I can't—"

I go quiet. I can't possibly let him know what I'm really thinking right now. The truth is almost too painful for me to admit to myself.

I can't have one more person in the audience watching me fail.

He sighs and I know he's not going to fight me leaving. He's too sweet for that...but that doesn't mean he won't still fight.

As if we're sharing a wavelength, he leans down, brushing his lips against mine. "What we have here is magnetic. I know you feel it too. And I can't let you just walk away. Give me your name."

I shake my head, lips pursed. It's easier this way. I won't get hurt this way. "My name is Mystery Girl."

He groans, kissing me for real, his lips working feverishly against mine. I let him lead, loving the taste of him. He breaks the kiss, sucking in air. "Give me your number, baby. Please—"

I silence him with my own kiss, my arms wrapping around his neck. He grunts in frustration, but kisses me back, pouring his need into me. I feel him hardening in his briefs. I want more of him, and I don't just mean sex. One more day wouldn't be enough. One week wouldn't be enough. I know with a surety marrow-deep that he's an addiction I'd never be able to break.

But I wasn't lying to him before. My life is in utter shambles. I can't start something new with a guy. I have to go home and pick up the pieces. I have to figure out if I even have a job come next week. For all I know, Doctor Halla already found my perfect replacement.

He breaks our kiss with another groan of frustration.

"I'm goin' for broke here, gorgeous. Just give me your state of residence. I can work with that."

I laugh. I can't help myself. He's just so genuine. He wants me, and he won't bother trying to hide it. But I'm not going to break. I can't. And I'm a zodiac girl, remember? My Mystery Boy is a Taurus through and through. He's attracted to all things love and sex. He's going to be bull-headed about this to the bitter end.

Unluckily for my sweet Taurus, I'm a double Cancer. I know when to draw a line in the sand, and it doesn't get crossed. It's time to retreat back in my shell. I might be crushed on the inside, but I won't let him see it. Whatever this is between us, he's not going to be the one to walk away first. It has to be me.

But I still have four hours.

I wrap myself around him, desperate to stay lost in his scent. "Please—"

"What do you need, baby?" he pants, our warm breath passing between our open mouths. "I'll give you anything. Say it, and it's yours."

I whimper. "Just make it all stop. Be here with me."

"I'm right here," he says. "I'm not going anywhere."

"Be with me. Give yourself to me. Take everything." I feel like I can't catch my breath. This is taking all the energy I have left. My heart is breaking.

"Okay, baby," he soothes. "Okay. Here, turn around."

I'm trembling in his arms as he turns me. He takes my hands and lifts them, pressing them palm-flat against the window. He's pressed in right behind me, his hands trailing down my arms, down my ribs, to settle at my hips. He kisses a line across my shoulder before I feel his voice in my ear.

"Look out the window, baby girl. Keep your eyes open.

Seattle is *our* place. Here in this room, in this city, nothing can keep us apart."

I let his words wash over me, warming me from the inside out as I look out at the blinking city lights.

His hands are roving, warming me up. "You're mine. My dream girl. My perfect mystery. Say it."

My hands are cold against the glass. It grounds me. I'm at a crossroads in life and in fact. The heat of his arms and the cold of the city. One door closes and another opens.

"Say it," he growls, his cock notching at my entrance.

I tip my head back with a desperate sigh, my eyes locked on the shape of the Seattle skyline and I sink my hips back against him, burying him inside me to the hilt. "I'm yours. Only yours. Nothing can keep us apart."

9

JAKE

I wake to the sound of my phone ringing. The ringtone is Tears for Fears. *Caleb*. Why is he calling so early? He must have forgotten about the time change. I'll call the asshole back later. I snatch blindly for the phone, clicking the side to dismiss the call. I don't want the sound to wake...*fuck*.

She still hasn't told me her damn name. Well, I'm done playing games. I'm breaking her this morning. I swear to god, this girl is not getting away from me.

I roll over, ready to pull her sweet body tight against my morning wood. Hopefully we have time for a quickie before our alarms go off at 7:00AM.

God, I can't remember the last time I had so much sex. And each time was more earth-shattering than the last. That last time, we fucked against the window. She screamed, clenching me so goddamn tight, and I came so hard I saw white spots.

Never in my life have I seen a girl literally dripping with my cum. Now I get why some guys have a breeding kink. I wasn't lying before. If this was Vegas, I'd be ringing down to the front desk asking for an Elvis minister.

We rinsed off in the shower, both of us standing sex drunk under the spray. Then we crashed in the bed. I think I was asleep before my head hit the pillow.

No way in hell am I letting her slip away. I'll be riding with her to the airport. Heck, I'll try to pull the I'm-a-famous-NHL-player card to get through security with her. If I've only got Seattle, I'm gonna milk every last second. I'm not giving up until the gate agent closes that door.

And I mean to play dirty. Anything to win. It's not like there's a penalty box she can shove me in. The first four words out of my mouth are about to be 'My name's Jake Compton.'

I reach for her, my hand snatching at the cold sheets. She's not in the bed. My eyes dart open, and I wince. Weak morning light streams in through the windows. I'm instantly on edge.

Something's wrong.

I roll over, twisting up in the sheets as I scramble for my phone. I tap the screen and my heart drops out of my chest. 8:37AM.

"No! No, no, no—fuck!"

She turned off my phone alarm!

I stumble my naked ass out of the bed, my gaze darting around the hotel suite. I already know what I'm going to find. Her suitcase is gone. Her discarded heels, her sexy black jumpsuit—gone. Her kindle was on the beanbag thing and there was a small pile of jewelry on the side table and an extra phone cord. All gone.

She's gone. Mystery Girl is gone.

She didn't even wake me to say goodbye. My heart cracks open in my chest.

I stumble across the suite into the bathroom and turn on the light. My breath catches as I see that she's left something on the counter. Oh god, it's a note. It's going to be her name and phone number!

I snatch up the piece of hotel stationary, but a quick scan has my heart sinking. No hint of a digit. No name. I lean against the sink and read:

Dear Mystery Boy,

Thanks for last night. You have no idea what it meant to me to share this perfect moment. I'm sorry I'm leaving without saying a proper goodbye, but it's better this way. As I packed, I thought of a poem by Rumi:

"The minute I heard my first love story,
I started looking for you, not knowing
how blind that was.
Lovers don't finally meet somewhere,
they're in each other all along."

Maybe we'll meet again. Maybe not. Either way, we've been in each other all along.

XO,

Mystery Girl

I glance back down at the sink. She left me something else. I set down the paper and pick up the thin vial of travel-size perfume. I unscrew the cap. One whiff and I'm groaning, dick twitching. It's *her* perfume. It's not a clue to her identity, but at least it's something, some piece of her, some proof that this was real. It happened. *We* happened.

I'm not giving up. I'm finding my Mystery Girl if it's the last thing I do. And when I find her again, I'm *never* letting her go.

To be continued...

Or keep swiping...

SNEAK PEEK: PUCKING AROUND

Swipe to read an exclusive first look at the first five chapters
of PUCKING AROUND!

CHAPTER 1

RACHEL

"R ACHEL!"

I groan, not ready to open my eyes and face the truth. It's morning. *Again.* And I'm officially going to murder my roommate Tess...just as soon as I remember how eyelids work. Why did I let her talk me into going out last night?

Because you're twenty-seven and single, girl. Live your damn life! I can hear her voice echoing in my head along with the steady *thump thump thump* of last night's dance music.

I'm pretty sure there was drinking last night. What else explains why my tongue feels superglued to the roof of my mouth? Oh god—I think I'm gonna be sick. I'm getting too old for this. I can't bounce back like I could when I was eighteen. There's only one solution: I'm just never drinking again. No more dancing. No more bars. Consider this my retirement from night life.

"*RA-CHEL!* Girl, get *up!*"

I roll onto my back, wincing as I gaze up at the blades of my slowly circulating ceiling fan. I think I slept with my contacts in. My eyes itch so bad.

Make a list, Rach. Make a plan.

That's been my mantra for the last two months as I've tried to put the pieces of my shattered life back together.

Hot shower, strong black coffee, maybe some eye drops—

"RACH!" Tess stomps down the hall and stands in the doorway, her wild, red curls spilling around her shoulders. She's a smokin' hot size twenty with a perfect, pear-shaped body. Per usual, she's wearing nothing but a crop top and her undies, a spray of peachy freckles dotting across her chest. The girl sheds clothes around this apartment like a husky sheds hair.

Not that I mind. I'm the daughter of a super famous rock star. Born in California and raised on a tour bus, I've seen some wild things in my time. A naked Tess doesn't bother me one bit.

"Girl, did you not hear me hollerin' for you?" She pops a hand on her hip and tosses my phone on the bed. "Someone's been trying to call you for like thirty minutes."

I reach blindly for it without turning my head. "Who is it?"

"I don't know. A New York number, I think. And there was a missed call from Doctor H."

I bolt upright, swallowing down the instant wave of nausea that hits me. "Ohmygod, Tess!" I snatch up my phone. "My boss is calling, and you let it just keep ringing?"

"Hey, I've got my own boss breathing down my neck, thank you very much," she says with a huff. "You handle *your* arrogant asshole, I'll handle mine." She flicks her hair over her shoulder as she turns. Her cheeky undies show off her freckled booty as she saunters away.

I roll my eyes, knowing she means well. Tess is just being overprotective because she's never liked Doctor Halla. She doesn't like the way he micromanages me or his cold, aloof manner. I guess it's just never bothered me. He can't help that he's European.

I drag a hand through my tousled hair, checking my text messages while I wait for my brain to warm up. Six texts and a missed call from my twin brother and his husband. I'm pretty sure Somchai is back in Seattle, which means this is early for him.

HARRISON (8:01AM): In NYC for cooking show. Wanna fly up for taping on Sat?

HARRISON (8:04AM): You *skull emoji*??

HARRISON (8:05AM): MISSED CALL

I grin, shaking my head. Just like a twin to give me exactly three minutes to respond to a question before he jumps to rigor mortis in his mind.

HARRISON (8:07AM): Hello *eyes emoji*

SOM (8:12AM): Girl, you better be dead bc your stupid brother just woke me up at 5AM. CALL HIM BACK

SOM (8:14AM): Plz don't actually be dead

HARRISON (8:20AM): I texted Tess and she says you're hungover, not *skull emoji* LMK about Sat

Now I'm laughing. These two are too much. My brother and his husband are rising stars in the culinary world. Apparently, Harrison was asked to be a guest judge on some new cooking show. He's always been more comfortable using our famous father's name and connections. I wouldn't be surprised if he drags him to the taping.

Which means that if I go, I'll be seated in daddy's shadow when the cameras inevitably pan to him for a closeup. Then I'll get three weeks of hassle as the tabloids remember I exist.

Yeah, no thanks.

I type out a quick reply in our group chat.

RACHEL (8:31AM): Not dead. Can't come bc I gotta work. But good luck *kiss face emoji*

Spotlight glare is literally the last thing I need right now because, two months ago, my own career rocket crashed out of the sky. I was in Seattle for Harrison's wedding when I got the news that I lost out on the Barkley Fellowship. The top sports medicine fellowship in the industry, it pairs early career doctors and physical therapists with professional sports teams. The last three residents Doctor Halla put up for it all won. After their ten-month rotations ended, they were all offered permanent positions.

I was supposed to be lucky number four. Doctor Halla was so sure I would win that he confidently started interviewing for my replacement in the residency program. I had to crawl back from Seattle with my tail between my legs and beg him not to give my spot away. He was kind about it, righteously indignant, swearing he'd never recommend a doctor to their sham of a program again.

So that's where I've been for the last two months, back in Cincinnati, going through the motions day to day. When I'm not putting in my residency hours at the hip and knee clinic,

I'm working out or hiding out...until Tess gets fed up and drags me out.

My therapist might be ready to prescribe Prozac, but Tess has a whole other kind of therapy in mind. Dick therapy. Since I got back from Seattle, she's been on a mission to get me laid. She thinks a wild night with a guy will cure me of my funk. But just the thought of touching another guy has me cringing.

I go still, my phone balanced in my hand.

Another guy. God, I'm such a mess. As if I already have a guy and Mr. Random Hookup would be the *other* guy. I don't have a guy. Not even close. But hey, a girl can dream, right?

In my case, my nightly dreams are full of only one guy. *The* guy. My Mystery Boy. I haven't told anyone about him. Not even Tess. We met on my last night in Seattle. It was the best one-night stand of my life. I've never felt so dialed in to another human soul before. But that's all it could be for me. One perfect night. No names. No numbers. I woke in the morning and quietly packed my bags, leaving him naked in my bed looking like my every dream.

I regret not telling him my name. He asked me to stay. He wanted me like I wanted him...*want* him.

I groan, dragging my hand through my messy hair again. I can't think about Mystery Boy right now. I've got to deal with Doctor Halla.

DR. HALLA (8:08AM): Price, call me ASAP

DR. HALLA (8:15AM): MISSED CALL

Taking a deep breath, I lift the phone to my ear and tap the little green call button. The dial tone chirps three times before it connects. "Dr. Halla, sorry I missed your call—"

"Price, are you here? Come to my office," he says in that posh, slightly accented voice.

"I—no, sir. I'm not scheduled to come in until this afternoon."

"Damn. Well, I didn't want to do this over the phone..."

I do a quick inventory. A shower is pretty much nonnegotiable. And I have to put some food in my stomach. And coffee. Lots of coffee. "Umm...I can be there in thirty minutes—"

"No. I don't want to keep them waiting."

Them? Why do I feel suddenly on edge? "Sir, what—"

"You got it."

My mind cranks like a pair of rusty gears as I try to puzzle out his meaning. "I—what?"

"The Barkley Fellowship. You got it," he repeats. His delivery is so deadpan that I'm not sure what to say. Is he joking? Because it's not funny. "Price? Did you hear me?"

"Yes." My heart is racing a mile a minute. "I don't understand—"

"I just got off the phone with Dr. Ahmed from the selection committee at the Foundation," he explains. "Apparently, you were first on the waitlist."

"Oh my god." I shove off the bed and stand on wobbly legs, looking helplessly around my room.

"Apparently, one of the fellows made the genius decision to go whitewater rafting and his raft flipped," Dr. Halla goes on. "Broke both his tibia and dislocated his shoulder, so he's out."

"Ohmygod," I gasp, pacing from the bed to the window. "So, what does that—"

"It means you're in," he replies, cutting right to the chase. "Dr. Ahmed called me as a favor. She knows you're my resident. She wanted to make sure you'd be serious about accepting. I told her you were. I hope I didn't over-step," he adds quickly.

"No, sir, I—" I hardly have words to speak. This can't be happening.

"You *are* still serious about it, right?"

"Of course," I all but shout into the phone. "I—this is just the last thing I expected. Didn't the fellowships already begin?"

"They only started this week," he replies. "That was the other reason she was calling. Usually, the fellows get some say in their placement. If not the specific team, then at the very least gender and sport. You'll need to be willing to fill this other fellow's place. It's already set up and it's too late to change it now."

Oddly enough, the total lack of control is giving me a kind of thrill. I feel like I'm skydiving. "Yes," I say. "I'll do it. Whatever it is, I'm in." I'm grinning now.

"Excellent," he replies. "It'll be more of a physical therapy role than primary care, but they're intrigued with your background in both. Dr. Ahmed wanted to check with me to make sure your experience at the clinic will translate well. I told her you're the perfect candidate."

My heart flutters. "Thank you, sir. Thank you so much for your support—"

"Say nothing of that," he says brusquely. He's not big on gushing. One of the residents hugged him at the Christmas party last year, and I thought he might turn to stone. "I believe Dr. Ahmed already tried to call you this morning. Call her back, and formally accept the fellowship. And don't worry about your shift this afternoon," he adds. "I'll apprise Wendy of the situation."

"Thank you," I stammer again.

"This is a great opportunity, Price. I'm pleased for you. Maybe you can get me tickets to a game this season."

His words register and I stop in my pacing. The fellowship started *this* week. Meaning I have to quit my job, pack up my life, and move, and I don't even know where I'm moving!

"Wait—what's the team?" I call out. "What sport? What city? Did she tell you?"

"Yes," he replies. "Your fellowship will be with the Jacksonville Rays."

My mind spins. Jacksonville. Atlantic side of Florida, I know that much. But my mind is drawing a blank at the Rays. The Jaguars are the NFL team...baseball maybe? God, if this is a test of my fit for their program, I'm utterly failing.

"I've never heard of the Rays," I admit.

He chuckles. "Well, you wouldn't. The Rays are the newest expansion team for the NHL. I don't think they've even finished the new arena yet."

I all but shriek with excitement, which is completely unprofessional, but I don't care.

Hockey. It's one of the most ruthless, injury-prone sports. The men play with literal knives strapped to their feet. Lots of bone breaks. Lots of shoulder, hip, and knee injuries. Dislocations. Groin pulls. It's my dream placement. And a new team means all new equipment, new facilities, over-eager fans.

"Sir—" I squeak out, unable to think of any other words.

He just chuckles again. "Have fun, Price. You've earned this." Then he hangs up.

I stand there with the phone in my hand, utterly speechless. I won the Barkley Fellowship.

Tess ducks her head back in my room, green smoothie in

hand. "You talk to Dr. H? What—girl, what's that smile? What happened?"

I start laughing, tears brimming in my eyes.

She pushes off the doorframe. "Girl, what—"

"I'm moving to Jacksonville," I blurt out.

"What—*when*?"

I wipe a tear from under my eye, shaking my head in shocked disbelief. "As soon as possible."

CHAPTER 2

RACHEL

"I don't know what else to tell you, ma'am. I'm looking at the screen, and I'm not seeing any record of your bags," the airline desk clerk drones for the third time.

I let out an exasperated groan, juggling my heavy backpack and purse on my shoulder while I snatch up the receipts on the counter. "Then explain *these*," I say, flapping them in the air. "The guy in Cincy checked all three of my bags. Clearly, they connected somewhere because—*look*—I've got one right here!" I gesture to the bag at my feet. It's one of Tess's old bags. The thing is holding itself together with little more than a prayer.

This is officially a disaster. The two missing bags have pretty much all my essentials. The bag I managed to claim was a last-minute pack job of odds and ends—a few medical textbooks, some bulky winter clothes, two evening gowns, and random workout stuff. I'm gonna look great waltzing into my first day of work tomorrow wearing a custom backless Chanel dress and my spin shoes.

"Can you *please* check again," I say, slapping the receipts back down on the counter.

It's been 32 hours of pure chaos. I'm hungry, I'm exhausted, and I'm feeling totally on edge after a long day dealing with multiple delayed flights. I didn't even sleep last night, too busy packing. I said a tearful goodbye to Tess before I was at the airport by 6:00AM for my first flight.

But a series of mechanical delays means it's now after 5:00pm, and I've only *just* landed in Jacksonville. And now this human gargoyle wearing a button on her vest that says 'I love corgis' is telling me my luggage has disappeared off the face of the earth.

"I don't understand how two bags can just go missing—"

"Oh…wait," she murmurs, the screen of the computer glowing in the reflection off her glasses. "Yeeep…here they are. I typed the flight number in wrong."

I stay very still. It's easier this way. I don't get a manager called on me this way…or a police officer. "Please just find them."

While she starts clicking away, I shift the bags on my shoulder, looking down at my phone. It's been blowing up since I stepped up to the counter. Apparently, it finally decided to wake up from airplane mode. All the messages come flooding in at once.

I'm sure Tess wants updates. There are a few messages in the Price Family group chat too. I also have a few messages from an unknown number. I read those first.

UNKNOWN (5:05PM): Hey, this is Caleb Sanford from the Rays. I'll be picking you up from the airport. I drive a blue Jeep.

UNKNOWN (5:15PM): I'm here. Outside door 2.

UNKNOWN (5:20PM): Can't sit much longer before the guy makes me go around again.

Shit. No one said there would be an airport pickup!

UNKNOWN (5:30PM): MISSED CALL

UNKNOWN (5:45PM): Look, I don't mean to be a dick, but I can't wait much longer. It says your flight arrived 45min ago.

UNKNOWN (5:47PM): This is Dr. Price, right?

"Oh my god," I cry, shifting all my stuff around on my shoulder.

Great, now I look like a total jerk that just ignores calls and texts for an hour, leaving people to wait on me. I need to call this guy back. I need to get out of this damn airport!

"Please," I say over the counter for what feels like the hundredth time. "If the bags aren't here, I can come back, but I can't just keep standing here—"

She raises a hand in my face. "Ma'am, I need you to calm down."

Oh, no she didn't.

"Calm down?" I seethe. "I haven't begun to be *un*-calm. You're the one who said my bags weren't even in the system two seconds ago—" I choke back the rest of my tirade. It's not worth it. "*Please*," I say again. "Just tell me—"

"Got it," she murmurs, her eyes back on the screen. "Looks like two of the bags were misdirected during your connecting flight in Charlotte. We can have them rerouted here sometime tomorrow morning."

I sigh with relief. "Thank god. What do you need

from me?"

"Nothing," she replies, sliding the bag receipts back across the counter at me. "We've got all your contact info. Someone will be in touch letting you know when the bags have arrived."

I snatch up the receipts. "Thanks," I mutter, only adding the 'for nothing' inside my own head.

"Welcome to Jacksonville," she deadpans, already waving at the next person in line.

I fight with the strap of my purse, which is now wrapped in my backpack strap and hooked around my metal water bottle. At the same time, I reach down for the handle of my checked bag. It's one of those boxy, black rectangles, lumpy down the front with all the odds and ends I've crammed inside. The thing weighs a ton! Whatever, it rolls. And now I'm on a roll.

I hurry away from the lost baggage desk, dragging my one lonely bag behind me. I've got my purse strapped across my body, so my left hand can be free. I'm already tapping the call button on my phone. It rings and he picks up immediately.

"Hello?" His voice is deep.

"Hi—" *Shit—what was this guy's name?* "This is Rachel Price," I say. "I'm *so* sorry! My bags are lost and then my phone was stuck on airplane mode—it was a whole thing. I'm coming out now!"

"I'm pulling around again," he says. I can hear music rocking in the background. "Blue Jeep." He hangs up.

I race over to the double doors marked with a big number 2 and rush outside. The Florida heat hits me like a slap to the face. I'm used to the dry heat of a California summer, not this swamp. Thank goodness my hair is already up in a knot. I've got to get this hoodie off pronto.

A topless, dark blue Jeep pulls to a stop at the crosswalk about ten yards away. A surfboard is strapped to the top rails, and a dog peeks his head out of the backseat. He's adorable—black pointy ears, with a white snout like a border collie. His pink tongue lolls from his mouth.

I run towards the Jeep, the wheels of my bag rattling against the cement. I lift my hand holding the phone, awkwardly waving the Jeep down. The guy in the driver's seat nods. He's wearing aviators and a ball cap with the brim pulled low.

"Hi," I say, breathless as I stop at the passenger side of the Jeep. "I'm Rachel Price. I'm *so* sorry again! My phone wasn't working, and two of my bags are missing, and I've been up for 36 hours, and I'm just a red-hot mess. But I'm here now, and I'm ready to go and—ohmygod, you are *so* cute—"

The guy in the front seat stiffens, his mouth opening a little in surprise, but I'm not actually paying attention to him. As I spilled my guts, the dog hopped between the seats, popping his face over the edge of the passenger door. He's got gorgeous icy blue eyes, so bright and curious. I'm a huge sucker for animals. I could never have one growing up with the way we always traveled, so now I become painfully awkward in social settings if there is a dog involved.

"Sy, back," his owner commands, cranking the Jeep into park.

The dog wiggles his whole body, his tail flapping in the guy's face before he hops dutifully into the backseat.

"Need help with your bags?"

"Oh, no. I can get it," I say, my eye going back to him.

Oh shit.

Here I am fawning over a cute dog when his owner is even cuter. He slips his aviators off, tucking them into the top of his t-shirt, and I get the full effect of those dark eyes and cheekbones for days. He's got a day or two of stubble along his jaw, and the sexiest bow pout to his lips.

"I—"

Girl, get yourself together.

I snap my mouth shut.

Shit, when did it open?

"I'm fine," I repeat. "Let me just..." I don't even bother finishing the sentence. I just duck my head in shame and move around the back of the Jeep.

"Here, let me," he calls out. "The door can get jammed sometimes." That's when he unfolds himself from the driver's seat and—oh my sweet heavens. He's sculpted perfection. I could see the shoulders from the Jeep, but I wasn't betting on the height too.

He's graceful as he moves, turning his back on me to fiddle with the door. Ink covers his right arm from the wrist up, disappearing under the sleeve of his t-shirt. Swirls of color and detailed patterns. He swings the door open, and I step back, ready to heft my bag inside.

"Here, let me get it," he mutters.

"No, don't bother." Why is my voice coming out so squeaky?

"That looks heavy."

"I'm a big girl," I reply, hefting it by the handle.

Then a few things happen at once. First, the car behind us honks, making me jump and the dog bark. Then the PA system starts blaring about parking in restricted areas. Lastly, as I lift the bag, I snag the edge of the door. This must have been just enough force to fray the ancient bag's last will to live. I hear the fabric tear, and then all hell breaks loose.

And by hell, I mean the contents of my bag. Yep, I stand

there, mouth open in horror, watching as all my belongings flood from the shredded canvas, spilling all over the curb at our feet.

Surfer Boy exchanges a wide-eyed look with me before we jolt into action, trying to catch all my falling stuff. I shriek as a book slams down on my exposed toes. This has me knocking back against the open Jeep door. Now the dog is barking in alarm, watching us scramble to keep my stuff from rolling into oncoming traffic.

Once we get the bag to the ground, I drop to my knees, desperate to shove everything back inside.

This is it. I've finally found it.

Hello, limit. I'm Rachel.

I work quickly, stuffing things back inside the broken bag. A few seconds pass when I realize Surfer Boy is just standing there, making no effort to help me. I glance up, my eyes trailing up his bare legs dusted with sand. Did he come straight from the beach? I pass over his board shorts, up his cut torso, to his face.

He's looking down, but he's not looking at me. No, he's looking at the thing in his hands. His expression is frozen on his face, totally unreadable.

And *thing* is right because—

Oh my fucking god.

My heart drops out of my chest. Someone bury me in the earth right here in this airport loading zone. And make sure to dig a hole for Tess right next to me, because I plan to haunt her to death! Surfer Boy is holding a dildo. *My* dildo. It was a gag gift from Tess, and it's most certainly a gag that she packed it for me. It has to be, because the dildo is large and purple and shaped like an octopus tentacle.

CHAPTER 3

I'm standing in the 'no parking' zone of the Jacksonville airport with a tentacle dildo in my hand. It's electric purple and rubbery, and I can tell from the weight its battery operated.

Holy fucking shit.

How the hell did I get here?

I've been waiting for this woman for almost an hour, getting myself more and more worked up about entitled doctor types who have no consideration for others. I was ready to hate her. Hell, I was ready to drive off and leave her ass here.

But then my phone finally rang, and this walking hurricane of a girl swept through the automatic doors, sucking me into her vortex. She talked at me so fast, I could barely make out the words. All I could do is watch the elegant arch of her throat as it moved. Then Sy had to go bouncing around, distracting us both.

She's gorgeous, I'll give her that. Her curvy body is clad in high-waisted black leggings and a cropped hoodie unzipped to show her cleavage. She did the world a favor by strapping her purse between her breasts and running towards me like a Baywatch model. Once she's close enough, I see the little glint of gold at her nose.

Fuck, she's got a septum piercing.

I'm a sucker for a pierced and tatted girl. Does she have tats too? I can't tell. What I can tell is that the guys are gonna go crazy. She'll be breaking hearts by day's end tomorrow. Coach is gonna have to put up an electric fence around her office. We'll probably have to make the rookies take cold showers before she examines them.

And here I am, still holding her dildo.

She's on her knees, scrambling to gather her shit, cursing under her breath. She looks up at me and I'm still just fucking standing here, like I've been turned to stone. Her dark gaze drops from my face down to my hand and her lips part in an "O."

"Oh my god," she shrieks, launching to her feet. "*Give* me that—"

She all but slaps the dildo out of my hand.

Say something, asshole.

"Just trying to help," I mutter, slipping my hands in the pockets of my board shorts, decidedly *not* helping. I'm afraid to help now. Afraid of what else I might find...what else I might touch. Does she actually use that thing or—

"It was a joke gift," she says quickly.

I hope she can't read my thoughts, because I won't deny the moment where I just pictured myself flipping that little switch and turning it on. I'm curious to test the toy's range of motion.

"My roommate's idea of a going away present," she adds, shoving the toy deep inside her bag. "I don't—I've never

—*god*, will you just get down here and help me before we get towed?"

I don't bother hiding my smirk. So, she's never used it before?

Don't go breaking my heart, Hurricane.

I bend my good knee, dropping down with a slight wince, and help her shove things back inside the broken bag. The rest of the plunder is innocent enough—books, random chargers, and cables. I pick up a snow boot. "You expecting snow on the beach?"

She huffs and grabs it, shoving it inside the split in the bag. "Always good to be prepared. Thought I might need to pack snow gear for an away game or something."

That's smart. I wouldn't want to be stuck with just my flip-flops in Toronto either.

We finish gathering her stuff quick as we can and team-lift the bag into the back of the Jeep. Whatever wouldn't fit back inside is tossed unceremoniously on top. She tucks her backpack safely in the backseat, keeping her purse with her as she climbs in the front.

I slide in on the driver's side and slip my sunglasses on. "Any preferences on the music?"

"No," she replies, helping herself to my phone charger. "Sorry, my battery is dying."

"Okay, well it's gonna get a bit windy," I say. "You might wanna—"

"I know how Jeeps work," she huffs, clicking her seatbelt on.

We both go still as we sit in the silence of her response.

Then she groans, burying her face in her hands. "Oh, shit—I'm so sorry. That was the bitchiest thing to say ever."

"It's okay—"

"No, I'm *so* sorry, I'm just—*god*—I'm so tired," she says, a note of desperation in her voice. "I think I might be getting a bit delusional."

I swear, if I have to deal with a tentacle dildo *and* tears in the same car ride, I'm gonna ask for a raise. Airport runs already aren't in my job description, but I'm trying to pull my weight, be a team player. Look what I get for my trouble.

"I haven't slept in like two days," she goes on.

Yeah, those are tears in her voice. I am now officially uncomfortable.

"And I'm so hungry. I haven't had anything but a bag of pretzels since this morning. But that's no excuse," she adds quickly. She turns to me, her fingers brushing lightly against the ink on my forearm. "I'm sorry. God, I'm such a mess that I don't even remember your name. I feel like a total bitch. You put it in your text, but I was in such a rush, and I couldn't check it again. And you were waiting for me for so long, and I'm sure you think I'm a total jerk, but I'm not—"

The words only stop because she's out of air. Yeah, this girl is a total swirling vortex of mass chaos.

She closes her eyes and takes a deep breath. Then she opens them, those dark brown pools sucking me in. "Can we start over? *Please*, let us start over." She holds out her hand to me. "I'm Rachel Price. I'm the new Barkley Fellow, and I've had a *really* rough two days."

I look down at her offered hand. She's tugged her hoodie sleeve up a bit and now I can see that she has tattoos.

Be still my cold dead heart.

A pair of hearts outlined on her wrist, a small, detailed sketch of an electric guitar on her forearm. There's a signature alongside the guitar.

Sy chooses this moment to pop his head between the

seats, nosing her open palm, which diffuses the tension. She giggles, giving him a pet between the ears. "At least someone wants to give me another chance. I swear I'm not a bitch. No, I'm not," she croons in that sugary sweet talking-to-a-dog voice all people seem to have. "No, I'm not. I'm really nice. Yes, I am."

Sy eats it up, licking her hand as she laughs out loud.

With a groan, I gently push him back and put out my hand, letting her shake it. "I'm Caleb Sanford, Assistant Equipment Manager."

She smiles. "Wow, tough job. You guys work crazy hard."

"Yep." I drop her hand, placing mine back on the wheel.

"And who is this angel?" she asks, turning in her seat to give Sy more attention. "His eyes are *so* gorgeous. I could just eat you with a spoon. Yes, I could," she coos.

The furry idiot is a total chick magnet. Too bad he warms them up only for me to put them right back on ice.

"His name is Poseidon," I reply. "I call him 'Sy' for short."

"Ooo, how regal," she says, her fingers scratching the thick fur of his neck. "You feel a bit salty, Sy. Were you swimming in the ocean with daddy earlier today?"

I go stiff.

Wait—no. My arms—my—*shit*, not my dick. My dick is definitely not going stiff at hearing a gorgeous woman call me 'daddy.'

With a groan, I turn away from her, my eyes firmly on the road as I jerk the Jeep into gear. At the same time, I crank up the radio, blasting the air with my favorite mix of rock music.

She fishes a pair of sunglasses out of her bag and slips them on, leaning back in her seat with a smile the moment we hit that Florida sunshine. Between the wind and the music, it's hard to have a conversation in a Jeep...which is one of the reasons I like driving with the top off.

She doesn't seem to mind. In fact, it seems to relax her. Within minutes. she's got one arm propped on the side door, her hand weaving to the beat of the music, as I coast us onto the interstate.

CHAPTER 4

RACHEL

"Well, here you are, hon. Home sweet home."

I follow the apartment manager inside the open door of my new apartment. My hands are full with my purse, my apartment paperwork, a drink cup sloshing with crunchy ice, and a bag of leftover tacos. I heft it all onto the kitchen counter, turning to face the view.

This is a fully furnished unit on the fourth floor of a brand-new complex not five miles from the arena. Caleb said the Rays bought out the top three floors of this building to have places to house rotating staff like me, as well as keep units in a constant state of readiness for farm team guys.

"You've got all the amenities," she says. "Dishwasher, stove, microwave are all here. And there's a small washer and dryer stack in your hall bath." She points to an open door.

I step past her into the living room. It's just a one bedroom, but there's a kitchen with a little breakfast bar and a narrow living room capped with a wall of glass that leads out to a balcony. Beyond the balcony, I can see I have a view of woods beyond.

"Bedroom is through here," Loretta calls. "You've got a full bath and the step-in closet."

I follow her into the bedroom, noting the beachy colors everywhere—nautical blue, sand beige, and white. Everything in the unit is accented with wicker and seashells. There's a jute rug in the kitchen. A sand dollar art print is framed over the queen-sized bed. Not a single decorating element is what I would have ever picked for myself. It's coastal chic and I love it.

Okay, I'll get used to it.

Fine, I'm buying a different bedspread at a bare minimum. Anyone who can handle this much sand beige must be part camel.

"It's perfect," I say.

Footsteps behind us have me turning. Caleb is standing in my kitchen, glancing around with a slight frown on his face. "Whoa...I forgot they look like this when you first move in."

"Like what?" I say, taking my heavy backpack as he hands it over to me.

He scrunches his nose. "Like aisle four of a Home Goods."

I stifle a laugh. Yeah, I'll be hiding at least a quarter of these decorations in a cabinet.

"Making new friends already?" Loretta calls. "Don't worry, hon. We're not all as surly as this one." She jabs a thumb at him.

Caleb picks up the glass bowl of seashells on my counter with a rattle. "Just curious, Lo, are there any shells actually left on the *beaches* here in Florida, or are they all in these fancy salad bowls?"

"You said something about recycling?" I say over him.

He smirks, setting the bowl back down.

"Yes, we recycle here. There's a laminated list on the counter of what needs to be separated out," Loretta explains. "And if you're caught breaking the rules, there's a $20 fine. The next fine goes up to $50."

"We take ocean conservation very seriously," Caleb chimes.

How the hell did he get around me and into the living room so fast?

"Take only photos, leave only footprints," he intones. At the same time, he's now holding what looks like a dried sea sponge decoration.

I roll my eyes at him. This guy is so hard to figure out. Is he an asshole or is he charming? Maybe he's a charming asshole. I smile, trying to focus on Loretta's long-winded explanation on proper dishwasher usage.

As she talks, I can't help but glance over at him. He's making himself at home on my sofa, moving around the striped pillows. He was so stand-offish at first. Understandable, since he thought I was standing him up...which I kind of was, totally inadvertently. Then there was the whole dildo debacle, which he was super cool about and hasn't mentioned again. On the drive he seemed distant. He clearly didn't want to talk, which suited me just fine. Especially since he's got great taste in music.

I thought I had him pegged as the surly asshole loner type. But then, just before we got to the apartment complex, he pulled into a little strip mall and bought me tacos.

"You said you were hungry," he said with an indifferent shrug.

Sure, we ate in silence, but it wasn't an awkward silence. We sat outside at a little metal café table, sharing our chips with a very happy Sy.

Whatever Caleb lacks in charm, his dog more than compensates.

"Oh, no—Sy," I cry, cutting Loretta off. "You can't leave him in the Jeep. Bring him up."

Caleb has his nose buried inside my coffee table book: *Florida's Seashells: A Beachcomber's Guide.* "It's okay," he replies, closing the heavy book and tossing it down. "I dropped him off when I brought up your backpack."

"Dropped him off?"

"Didn't this grumpus tell you?" Loretta laughs.

I glance between him and Loretta. "Tell me what?"

Caleb crosses over to me. "I'm your new neighbor, Doc."

My heart skips a beat. "Neighbor?"

"Yep, he's right next door in unit 403," calls Loretta.

"Why else do you think I was volunteered to pick you up from the airport?"

I gaze up into his dark eyes and feel something in my belly swoop. And no, it's not the tacos. Oh, this is so not happening. No way.

Red alert. Back up, Rachel. Shut it down.

I'm not getting involved with a coworker. I don't care if he's gorgeous and working a smolder so hot it burns.

"So, if you ever need some sugar," he murmurs. "You know who to ask."

CHAPTER 5

RACHEL

I sigh with exhaustion, swaying at my kitchen counter as I pour myself a generous glass of chardonnay. I successfully made it to the end of this marathon two days. At this point, I'm not sure which I need more: sleep or air. It's a toss-up, really. As soon as I down this wine, I plan to crash.

Once Caleb left, I unpacked my one ridiculous bag, confirming what I already knew. The only choice in clothes for tomorrow are two evening gowns, a couple bikinis, a white lacy swimsuit coverup, or my winter gear. So, I called for an Uber and made a Target run. Three hours and $600 later, I was back in my apartment with a stocked fridge and pantry, a new comforter on the bed, new pillows on my sofa, and a load of laundry spinning in my mini washer—to include new scrubs and underwear.

Just as soon as the washer buzzes, I'll toss the clothes in the dryer and go to sleep.

I fiddle with my phone, turning on some music. I stripped my leggings off as soon as I got home. Sports bra too. So now I'm wearing nothing but my undies and the softest cropped band tee I found in the junior's section.

Grabbing my phone and my glass of wine, I saunter across my apartment towards the balcony. I'm a snob about making my outside spaces comfortable, and I'm already planning a patio makeover for this weekend—a plush lounger, some cafe string lights, plants for the railing. I could have one just for herbs. Basil and dill, maybe some rosemary. I make a note on my phone, using my elbow to slide the glass door shut behind me.

It's so lovely out here. The humidity from the day has finally cut, so now it's just warm. And so blissfully quiet. My music plays as I scroll mindlessly on my phone, slow sipping my chardonnay. I'm a few pages into my latest monster romance when I hear the loud buzzer on my washer go off. Draining the rest of my wine, I go to open the sliding glass door.

Shunk.

It doesn't budge.

"Oh, you gotta be kidding me," I mutter. I tuck my phone under my arm and give the handle a harder pull.

Shunk. Shunk. Shunk.

"Oh, no. Fuck, fuck, fucking fuck!" I hiss, setting both the phone and the empty wine glass down. "Come on, door. Please, don't do this to me," I whine, trying to see if there's something I'm missing, some lever that need lifting or a latch that needs flipping. But no. Nothing. There is literally nothing on this side of the glass except the handle.

"Oh, come *on*!" I snatch up my phone and go quickly through my contacts, looking for the number to the front office. Of course, I haven't plugged it into my damn phone yet!

"This is just perfect," I mutter, opening my internet to do a google search.

I swear to god, when I get myself out of this, I'm going to

bed and I'm never waking up again. I jerk the phone up to my ear, waiting as the dial tone plays some shitty elevator music. After what feels like an eternity, an answering service finally connects.

"Thank you for calling the Silver Shells Maintenance Service. Our office is currently closed. If this is an emergency, please hang up and dial 911—"

I hang up.

Oh god, I am *not* calling the police to come rescue me! I have a sudden image of a firetruck raising up a ladder to my fourth-floor balcony. A handsome fireman reaches out his hands, ready to lift me over the rail like I'm a kitten stuck in a tree. I'm sure all my new neighbors will enjoy watching me shimmy my bare ass over the balcony into a fireman's ladder-bucket-thingy.

I gasp.

I know my new neighbor!

I glance over the edge of my balcony towards Caleb's unit. Less than two feet of space separates our railings. The angle isn't quite right for me to see inside his unit, but I can tell that a light is on.

"Please, oh please," I mutter, pressing the call button on his contact.

It rings and rings. No answer.

"No," I whine, dropping the phone to both hands to shoot off a text.

RACHEL (11:04PM): Hey Caleb, this is Rachel. Are you home? I see the light is on. Can you come out onto your balcony?

RACHEL (11:04PM): Right now. It's kind of an emergency.

I wait, desperate to see the three little dots flashing at the bottom or—better yet—hear him open his sliding glass door.

Nothing.

RACHEL (11:06PM): Caleb please! I'm stuck out on my balcony!

I keep waiting.

Nothing.

Oh god, my heart is starting to race with anxiety and now I *really* have to pee!

Going for broke, I take a deep breath and start calling his name. "Caleb Sanford! Hey, Caleb!"

I wait.

"Caaaaaleb!"

Inside his unit, I hear Sy barking.

"Yes, help me, Sy!" I call out like an idiot. "Get daddy's attention for me! CALEB!"

And *whoosh* goes my relief with the sound of his sliding glass door as it opens. Sy hops out, his little black and white head darting between the railing bars as he barks over at me.

"What the—"

"Caleb!" I call again. "Oh, thank god."

"Rachel?" He peeks around the corner at me. He's shirtless, his coppery hair mussed. I can see that his tattoo sleeve goes all the way up his arm, over his shoulder. The rest of him is long and lean, cut with muscle. "What are you—"

"Do you ever check your phone?" I cry, cheeks burning with embarrassment.

He raises a confused brow. "It's in my room. Rachel, what the—"

"I'm locked out," I blurt.

"What?"

"I came out on my balcony, and I shut the door behind me, and apparently it locked!"

He chuckles, dragging a hand through his messy hair. "Oh yeah, Lo should have warned you. Don't shut the door all the way unless you wanna get locked out."

I deadpan at him. "Yeah, gee, thanks. I think I've learned that lesson. Now, can you *help* me?"

He glances around. "Well...did you call the maintenance number?"

"The office is closed. The auto message said to call 911."

"That's probably your best option. They can unlock your unit and get you free."

I whimper, already moments away from doing the pee dance. "But that'll take *ages*."

He smirks. "You got somewhere fancy to be?"

I freeze.

Of fucking course.

If I can see him standing there in nothing but his shorts, he can see me in my thong and cropped Guns N' Roses tee. I cross my arms over my braless tits. No way is he getting more of a show from me today. He's seen my dildo and now he's seen me in my underwear. He's not getting a glimpse of the girls too.

"I can keep you company if you want," he says with a shrug. "While you wait for the police."

I groan again. The last thing I want is to sit up here, possibly for hours, waiting for the police to force entry into my unit and come free me from this balcony prison. If that happens, they're going to find a sobbing mess of a woman sitting in a puddle of her own pee.

And that's when the world's worst, most genius idea slips into my head. "Or…"

"Or what?" Caleb replies, one elbow leaning on his rail.

I judge the distance. Not even two feet, with more than enough space where both our balcony railings extend out. Easy peasy. Just don't look down. "Or I could just climb over there."

He blinks at me. "The fuck you say? We're on the fourth floor. You fall, you fall to your death, Doc. Splat."

"I'm not going to fall," I huff. "Look, just extend out your arms and we can better judge the distance—"

"No," he barks, taking a step back. "No fuckin' way. I'm not gonna help you ninja crawl your way over here. How would that even help? You'd still be locked out."

"But you've got a bathroom," I plead. "And if worse comes to worst, maybe I could crash on your couch and maintenance can open the door for me first thing in the morning. That way we don't have to involve the police. *Please*, Caleb—"

"You're fuckin' crazy, Hurricane," he mutters, shaking his head. "I'm not helping you. No is my answer. Don't even ask."

I whimper, hands dropping to my sides. Oh god, I can feel the tears coming. Once the lower lip starts quivering, there's no stopping it. And I'm not a crier. This has just been a ridiculously stressful two days.

"Oh, what is that?" he growls, tone wary.

I sniffle. "Nothing. It's fi-fine."

Oh god, this man is going to *hate* me. Between the way we met and my dildo surprise and now this, I wouldn't blame him if he never speaks to me again. And we have to work together! He was giving me a ride to the arena in the morning.

Now he's standing there like a handsome, bare-chested Hercules, leaning over his railing, looking at me like I'm a three-headed hydra.

"Don't." He shakes his head. "Please don't do that. Don't fuckin' cry. I can't stand when people cry—"

"I can't help it," I snap at him. God, I can't let him watch me fall apart. I duck away from the railing's edge, using our shared wall as a barrier as I fall quietly to pieces.

After a minute, he groans and Sy whimpers. "Come on...Rachel?"

"It's f-fine," I garble. "I'll be fine. Just g-go back inside. I'll call the p-police and wait h-here."

I can hear him muttering to the dog. "God—*fuck*—fine!" he shouts over at me. "Rachel, I'll help you."

I go still. "You will?"

"Yes—fuck," he mutters again. "But if you fall and die, I'm telling the police that a crazy woman was trying to break into my apartment."

I wipe my nose with the back of my hand, sniffing back my tears. "That's fair," I call over. "Here—take my phone first." I reappear at the balcony's edge, leaning over with my arm outstretched, phone in hand.

He reaches it easily. See? This is totally gonna work. He takes it and slips it in the pocket of his shorts. His mouth is set in a grim line. "How do you wanna do this, Doc?"

I survey the scene. "Umm...I think if I sort of climb up, I can reach out with one hand." I mime as I talk. "Then maybe you can support me as I let go and reach out with the other. Then I'll sort of just jump over, and you reel me in. Thoughts?"

"Yeah, I think this is the stupidest fucking idea ever."

I scowl at him. "Shut up, we're doing it."

"Why can't you just sit over there and wait for the police?"

"Because," I huff, testing out the railing as I shimmy my way up.

"Because why?"

"Because I'm taking back control of my life!" I shout. "In the last 36 hours, I've gone from wallowing in the depths of a depression thinking I didn't win this fellowship to learning that I did." I climb up, using all my yoga balance to cling like a monkey to the bars of my railing.

"I packed up my life, said goodbye to my best friend, moved to a state and a city I don't know, to take a job I'm not sure I can do, with a team I've never met," I go on with a huff, carefully letting go of the wall to reach out my hand towards him.

He's there in an instant, his warm hand wrapping tight around my wrist, providing me balance and support.

"I've survived flight delays and missing bags. I had a stranger fondling my dildo in public—a dildo I totally use, by the way," I add as I fling my other arm out towards him.

"Shit—*fuck*—" he grunts, his hands going from my wrists to just under my ribs as he takes a death grip hold of me. "Wait—seriously?"

"Yeah, I was lying before," I reply. "And before you ask, yes it vibrates and *yes* it feels amazing. And now we are never going to talk about it again. *Ever*. Do you understand me?"

"*Ungh*—yeah—"

We're both panting as I'm now in a kind of stretched-out downward dog pose, with my feet pressed against the top of my balcony railing and my hands gripping tight to his bare shoulders.

He shifts his hold on me and stills. "Uhh...Doc?"

"Yeah?" I pant, wiggling my toes and doing my best not to look down.

"My hand is umm..."

"Totally grabbing my bare tit?" I finish for him. Because yeah, this crop top is too big, and his hand just slipped right under the bottom hem. He's got a fierce hold on my ribcage, and I can feel his thumb brushing the underside of my boob. "Yeah, I got that Caleb, thanks. Just pull me the fuck over. Ready?"

"Yeah—*shit*—please don't die—"

"Please don't drop me," I echo. "3-2-1-*go*!"

I push off with my toes and his arms snake around me tighter than a vice, pulling me across the void. His skin is hot, and his breath is in my ear, as one arm bands tighter at my shoulders and the other drops down, his strong hand at my waist.

I cry out as my shins whack into his railing, but he gets a hand on my butt and lifts me up and over to safety. He stumbles backwards as I go full koala on him. We're wrapped in an embrace more intimate than what I've shared with some of my former lovers. I don't know where his skin ends and mine begins. We cling to each other, heart's racing, as Sy dances around at our feet.

"Uhh...Doc?" Caleb says after a minute, his breathe warm in my ear.

I huff a tight laugh. "Your hand is cupping my bare ass? Yeah, I know. Thanks for the play-by-play, Sanford. Why don't you put me down now."

He grunts, loosening his hold on my bare ass cheek. I un-koala myself, sliding down his front with my whole body as he sets me on my feet. We stand there, both still shaking, my hands on his shoulders and his hands on the bare skin of my waist.

There's an energy sparking between us. It makes me nervous. I haven't felt it since—

No, don't go there.

I can't do this again. I can't let my ridiculous notions about vibes and energy drag me down yet another path to heartache. Mystery Boy was a one-time encounter. Earth-shattering sex? Yes. Soul-shattering to leave the next morning? *Hell,* yes.

Caleb is different. This has to be different. I know him and he knows me. We're about to work together. Heck, my contract is already signed. We *do* work together. This is wrong. This is dangerous. This is not happening.

I inch away from him, my body stiff.

"Are you okay?" he murmurs, his hand raising to brush softly along my jaw.

I close my eyes at the gentle touch. "Don't be nice to me," I murmur. "Please—"

He stills. Then his hand is under my chin, tipping it up. "Look at me, Hurricane."

Hurricane? Is that supposed to be me? Why does the nickname make my pulse flutter?

I open my eyes and glance up at him. The light from his apartment is soft, casting half his face in shadow. He's beautiful. Those sharp cheekbones and dark eyes put me in mind of a fae prince, cold and mysterious. Not to mention those pouty, kissable lips.

"Are you okay?" he repeats.

I nod. Then after a moment, I shake my head.

I don't even know how it happens, but in moments I'm back in his arms, crying against his chest as he holds me, his hand soothing down my back. I cling to him as I let loose all my exhaustion and stress and pain. When nothing is left to feel, only one thought remains.

"You wanna talk about it?" he murmurs.

I let out a soft sigh, my body relaxing against him. "I miss him."

He stiffens slightly. "Miss who? Your boyfriend?"

I shake my head. No. Not my boyfriend. Not my anything.

"Your husband?"

I smile, pushing off his chest. "Nope. Never married."

"Me neither. Brother then?"

I laugh, shaking my head again. "No. He's...no one," I reply, even as my heart says the word I really mean.

Someone.

He's my someone. Somewhere out there, he's being a whole person. And I'm here, afraid to let myself give in to the energy sparking between me and this beautiful man. Who knows, maybe this surly equipment manager is meant to be my *new* someone.

But I'm not ready for new. I'm not ready for any of the changes life has suddenly thrown my way. And yet, I have to find a way to fake it until I make it, because my life is happening right now. I've got the throbbing shins to prove it.

"Come on," Caleb says, offering out his hand. "You're dead on your feet, Doc. Let's get you set up on the sofa, huh? Live to fight another day."

Nodding, I take his hand.

ALSO BY EMILY RATH

SECOND SONS SERIES

Spicy 'why choose' Regency Romance

#1 BEAUTIFUL THINGS

#2 HIS GRACE, THE DUKE

#3 ALCOTT HALL

STANDALONES

Contemporary MM Omegaverse

WHISKEY & SIN

JACKSONVILLE RAYS SERIES

Spicy hockey romance

#0.5 THAT ONE NIGHT

#1 PUCKING AROUND

#2 PUCKING WILD (coming Summer 2023)

#3 PUCKING SWEET (coming Fall 2023)

Additional Content

#1.5 PUCKING EVER AFTER: VOL

LEMONGRASS (A Jax Rays novella exclusive to the Queer & Cute
Anthology coming June 2023)

ABOUT THE AUTHOR

Emily Rath is a romance and fantasy author. A university professor by day, she lives in Florida with her husband, son, and cat. They regularly comb the local beaches looking for shark teeth.

- Join my FB Group for exclusive first looks at art and new projects
- Join my Newsletter to get all my publishing news

Printed in the USA
CPSIA information can be obtained
at www.ICGtesting.com
LVHW081344070923
757406LV00006B/614

9 798987 793350